Mike Stovell was born to a poor but loving working-class family at the end of WW2 in the small town of Rugby in Warwickshire. Educated at three Victorian state schools, caned on a regular basis mainly for showing off to his classmates, he couldn't wait to leave school at the age of 15. He has led an exceptional and varied working life: a fireman on steam engines, an overhead linesman on pioneering electrification of the railways, a lorry driver, a publican, a market trader, an art dealer, an estate agent, and a housing developer, making and losing millions – but he still describes himself as a rich man, because he knows money isn't everything. You name it, he has done it, and you will see once you've shared his adventures that he is truly a loveable chancer that inspires hope and optimism in everything he does.

Mike Stovell

THE FINAL DEMAND

AUSTIN MACAULEY PUBLISHERS
LONDON · CAMBRIDGE · NEW YORK · SHARJAH

Copyright © Mike Stovell 2025

The right of Mike Stovell to be identified as author of this work has been asserted by the author in accordance with sections 77 and 78 of the Copyright, Designs and Patents Act 1988.

All rights reserved. No part of this publication may be reproduced, stored in a retrieval system, or transmitted in any form or by any means, electronic, mechanical, photocopying, recording, or otherwise, without the prior permission of the publishers.

Any person who commits any unauthorised act in relation to this publication may be liable to criminal prosecution and civil claims for damages.

This is a work of fiction. Names, characters, businesses, places, events, locales, and incidents are either the products of the author's imagination or used in a fictitious manner. Any resemblance to actual persons, living or dead, or actual events is purely coincidental.

A CIP catalogue record for this title is available from the British Library.

ISBN 9781037102066 (Paperback)
ISBN 9781037102073 (ePub e-book)

www.austinmacauley.com

First Published 2025
Austin Macauley Publishers Ltd®
1 Canada Square
Canary Wharf
London
E14 5AA

This is a story about two company directors of a high-end house-building company, who have had great success over twenty-five years winning local and national awards for their innovation within the industry. They are halfway through their biggest site so far when the 2008 so-called credit crunch rears its ugly head. Their bank, which proudly featured them on their last year's calendar, are now treating them like lepers.

It is Saturday morning in the boardroom. Frank Harrison is the first arrival for the almost pointless Saturday morning meeting. Frank is the more serious of the two directors, whereas Jack Redman is the joker in the pack; he would laugh if his arse was on fire. Frank, with his head in his hand, is poring over bills demanding money they haven't got when Jack the Joker walks in. "Good morning, Frank, and how are we today?"

"We are not good, that's what we are. We have got more fucking bills coming in and no bloody ammunition to pay them with, that's the problem, Jack. What the fuck are we going to do? The bank are taking the piss the way they are treating us, the bastards. All the bloody money they have had off us over the years, interest charges, set-up fees, completion fees, and now the bastards are throwing us to the lions. What the fuck can we do, Jack?"

"Well, Frank, there isn't much we can do. I am afraid the end is nigh. The only way out of this fucking mess is a lottery win, or we rob a bank."

"Don't take the piss, Jack; you can never take anything seriously!"

"I am being serious, Frank."

"Oh, yes, and I am sure we could get away with robbing a bank."

"I think we would stand a bloody good chance, Frank. The one thing we are experts at is planning, and that's what it would take: meticulous planning and military execution."

"Don't be bloody daft; we are builders, not fucking bank robbers. Get a grip, Jack."

"Frank, I am being serious. Do you remember me telling you about the time I met John Brown's brother-in-law when John was the landlord of the Fox at Pailton?"

"No, I don't remember; you're always meeting people in pubs."

"Well, let me tell you. I was enjoying a pint while chatting with John when his brother-in-law walked in. John introduced me to him, and it turned out that he was stopping with John for the weekend with his wife and family. We shared a few pints and a lot of small talk, and it came up he was a police officer in the flying squad in London. Over a game of pool and another couple of drinks, I asked him if his job was as exciting as it appears on the telly. He said, 'Not at all; in fact, it's boring. Believe it or not, most of our time is spent keeping an eye on known criminals. We spend most of our time in pubs and clubs or sitting in cars and vans, just looking and listening or talking to our snouts who are usually full of shit.' Then I asked him what would happen if a gang from a small town in the midlands that weren't known criminals and had no criminal records travelled to London or any big city and did a robbery, do you think they could get away with it? And his reply, much to my surprise, was, 'If you got away clean and you didn't kill anybody, and you didn't start chucking money around, then we could only do the usual; we would circulate the job to all the big cities, and we would call on all our snouts to see if there was any buzz going around. If there were no clues to go on after a couple of months, it would go on the unsolved crime register, and that's pretty much the end of the matter.' So, I reckon we would have a fair chance of getting away with it. What do you think, Frank?"

"I think you are becoming unhinged due to all this shit we are going through. I can't believe you're even thinking about it; it's a fucking ridiculous idea. You have come up with some things over the years, but this one takes the biscuit."

"It's not so fucking ridiculous; as a matter of fact, I have been thinking about it for the last couple of months. Just think for one minute, Frank. One bank job could save us from losing everything we have worked for over the last twenty-five years. And at the same time, give the great British banking system a swift kick in the bollocks that it well deserves by the way they are treating us, and not only us, all of the house builders are in the same boat. Come on, Frank, let's give it some thought at least."

"You're serious about this? No, Jack, don't fuck about. Get your head out of the clouds. We have got to sort this fucking mess out. Look at all these final demands. What are we going to do?"

"There is nothing we can do. The bank has stopped releasing money. As I said, Parker Lake Homes Ltd is a basket case. It's heartbreaking that after all these years some banker, or should I say, wanker, in a glass tower in London can put a line through a page and just like that finish us after all these years and after all we have been through. They're the fucking criminals.

"Come on, Frank, we are experts at planning. If we planned a bank job with meticulous attention to detail like we do with our houses, surely, we would stand a good chance of getting away with it. For fuck's sake, Frank, we can't just throw the towel in; we have got to fight back like we have always done."

"I suppose you're right there, Jack. We are fighters, but the bastards have got us on the ropes this time, that's for sure. All right, let's plan it just for a bit of light relief. Just plan, Jack, that's all. Don't let's get carried away. I know you; once you get excited, there's no stopping you. At least we will see if it is really viable, and it will take our minds off the shitstorm we are going through now."

"Yes, Frank, a bit of escapism will do us the world of good; at least it will take our minds away from all this load of bollocks." Jack picks up a handful of red letters and throws them across the boardroom table.

"Well, Jack, there's no time like the present. Where do we start?"

"Well, I suppose the first thing is to find a bank to rob and work back from there. What do you think, Frank?"

"Yes, you're right; that's the way we work. We find a site and start the planning process from there. This is no different when you think about it. So, let's both have a look on the internet through the week and see what we can come up with.

"Well, it's a start, Jack, but just remember from now on this is just a plan, and it must be kept close to our chests. If anybody, even our wives, knew about this, they would think we were having some kind of nervous breakdown; it must be our secret."

All the next week, Jack and Frank spend their evenings browsing the internet, looking for their target bank. On Thursday evening, Frank finds something interesting: a bank in Islington that is a type of sorting office for old notes, checking if the quality of the note is good enough to stay in circulation or if it needs to be incinerated. It looks good, so he phones Jack.

"Jack, I have found a strong possibility."

"Where is it, Frank?"

"I will tell you tomorrow at the office; loose lips sink ships and all that bollocks. See you tomorrow."

"Okay, mate, you're quite right about loose lips; see you in the morning."

The next morning, Jack walks into Frank's office. "Good morning, Frank."

"There's fuck all good about it, Jack. Look at this lot: bills and demands; the VAT is overdue. The bank has sent us another of their polite bollockings. I would like to get hold of that little bastard we went to see in London who said he sympathised with our position and would assist us where he could. The lying little bastard, I would like to assist him off the top floor of that fucking glass palace he sits in all day, assassinating honest businesses like ours. Anyway, enough of my ranting."

"Well, Frank, that's even more reason why we should concentrate on the bank job; at least it's constructive and not destructive. Anyway, what have you found that's got you so excited?"

"I have found a bank in Islington that carries out quality control on banknotes, checking whether they can stay in circulation or not. One big advantage that springs to mind is that there are no consecutive serial numbers on the notes. By the way, I was thinking about the weight of the money we are thinking of relieving the bank of. We need to know how much we can physically *carry*. We don't want to be millionaires with hernias, do we, Jack?

"It's a good thought, Frank. It's that sort of detail that will make the job a winner. But the hernia thing, I think if it did happen, we could afford a couple of young nurses to see us through the op and the recovery; you know, a nice bit of physio."

"Stop fantasising, you daft bugger; we must concentrate if this plan has any chance of working."

"I was only joking, but it was a nice thought while it lasted. If nothing else, this planning lark is taking our minds off the state of the business."

"I think we should have a code word for the job, Jack, in case there is something urgent that crops up and we need to talk privately."

"Good idea; it's all about detail. I am really beginning to enjoy this; it's getting more interesting by the minute. There is so much more to it than meets the eye, but the secret is first-class planning. So, let's both make a list of all the things we think we have got to do for a successful mission and how we achieve them."

"Yes, you are right, Frank, but before we get spending too much time and money, we can ill afford this. Don't you think we should go to London and have a look at this bank? Because if it looks like Fort Knox, we might as well forget the idea or start looking at something else."

"Yes, you're right there, Jack; we should do that. It would be madness to spend weeks planning something that can't work. We will go and have a look before we go much further."

The next morning, Jack and Karen, the secretary, are talking in the reception office.

"Karen, Frank and I are going to London in the morning to visit the building exhibition at Earl's Court. Ring me if you have any trouble. Mike will be in his office if you need any help for any reason."

"Okay, Jack, I should be all right if I have got Mike with me; he is a big lad."

"Oh, yes, and how do you know that, Karen, you naughty girl?"

"Not that kind of big lad, you cheeky sod. It will be nice having you two buggers out of my way for a day. I can catch up on the VAT returns, not that we will pay it- or not yet anyway. Well, have a nice day in London; it will do you both good to get away from here for a day with all the crap you are having to deal with."

The next morning, Frank meets Jack early at the noisy Rugby railway station. It is a shitty rainy morning with a very Dickensian feel about it. Frank has bought cheap day return tickets to Euston, second class, of course, given their present circumstances.

"How are you doing, Jack? I can't believe you have got me doing this. We must be mad going to London to case a bank."

"Well, I can't believe we are doing it either, but I'm bloody excited; it's a great distraction from all the stress we are going through with the business."

"Yes, you're right, Jack; even if we don't go through with it, it's great therapy for the financially challenged and the constantly hounded. It is bloody exciting; we have done some crazy things over the years, Jack, but this most definitely takes the Oscar. I don't know how you talked me into this, but I must admit, it is giving me a buzz, almost like when we first started the business together. It's a bit like starting all over again."

"I know what you mean, Frank. I have felt a bit like that; it feels as though we are starting a new business. So, what the fuck, let's get on with it. It can't do any harm at this stage; we haven't done anything wrong yet, except tell Karen a pack of lies. Mind you, that's nothing new."

"Come on, Jack; the train is on the platform."

The cheeky pair of buggers settle into first-class seats having bought second-class tickets, both fully convinced that a guard couldn't possibly check all the tickets on the train in fifty-three minutes. Both sit enjoying a complimentary cup of coffee and the opulence of their first-class coach. And then…

"Fuck me, Jack, here comes the guard checking tickets! I didn't think he would have time to cover the whole train on a short journey like this; he must have a rocket up his arse! I'm off to the toilet."

It's too late for Jack to do the same brainwave as the guard gets nearer, shouting, "Tickets, please!" He grabs his mobile phone and pretends to have a row with his wife.

"No, there is no other woman! I can't afford you with your extravagant ways, let alone another one like you. I am telling the truth. On my mother's life! Yes, I know she is, but if she were alive!"

The guard looks at Jack, looks up towards the ceiling, rolls his eyes, and walks on.

Jack sighs and thinks, *Fuck me, that was close.*

Frank comes cautiously out of the toilet, looking both ways, and makes his way back to his seat.

"Did he get you? I never thought he would get down this end of the train that quick."

"No, he didn't, but no thanks to you, you arse, leaving me in shit like that. You were faster than a parking warden's pen going into that bloody toilet."

"How did you manage to get away with it? You must have pulled a hell of a stroke. I was sure he would have had you."

"Gut reaction. I pulled out my phone at the speed of light and pretended to have a row with my wife."

"Brilliant! What a great move! He must have a nagging one at home. That gave you the sympathy vote. But, Jack, that sort of quick thinking can save the day. Well done, old chap."

"Yes, and it wasn't any thanks to you that I wasn't bloody well done."

They both laugh.

Jack and Frank get off the train at Euston, have a cup of tea, some toast and a chat.

"What if our lovely wives knew what we were up to, Frank? Casing a bank, I can hardly believe it myself. So, hopefully, nobody else will. Anyway, the building exhibition is a very good cover, not that we will be building anything anytime soon or even in the distant future, for that matter. What a complete balls-up these fucking banks have caused us and lots of others like us, the bastards. Every time I think about it, it spurs me on to really do this bloody bank job."

"If we did this and we got away with it, we wouldn't have to worry about building anything ever again. It would be off to sunnier climes for me. Spain, here I come! How about you? Where would 'Jack the Lad' fancy living? Would you come to Spain with me, Jack?"

"No, not Spain for Jack the Lad. I fancy Northern Cyprus; that would do me. Plenty of sunshine and cheap Turkish beer, not to mention belly dancers and no extradition laws. My mate who lives there will sort me out a top-quality villa and a car. He is a great guy."

"Come on, Jack, let's stop daydreaming and get back to reality. I don't suppose we will do it anyway, let alone get away with it."

Jack and Frank get a taxi to Islington to find their target bank.

"Thanks, driver, keep the change." They get out of the taxi, and Frank looks disappointed. "It doesn't look good; it's too exposed to the public, and there are guards on the door. This is not what we had hoped for."

"No, Frank, it's not what we expected, but surely this can't be where they do the recycling. There is nowhere they could load and unload on this busy street. Let's have a look around the back; we might have better luck there."

Jack and Frank walk around the back in disappointed silence, then Jack says loudly, "This looks more like it, Frank. It's completely different from the front; in fact, it's scruffy by comparison and not at all high-tech. Hang on, is that an armoured truck going in?" Frank notes the time of arrival down, watching every move.

They watch the guard get out and go to the intercom. He says, "First delivery, darlin'." Then he says the password, which they overhear to be 'Eagle'. The guard says, "Hi, Julia, open the gates; we are coming in."

Julia says, "Okay, lads, the pallets are ready on the loading bay, and I expect you would like a cup of tea."

"Yes, please, darlin'; we haven't had one yet today."

The truck drives in and reverses onto the loading bay. The driver and the guard jump out.

Julia opens the side door, walks out and says, "Sign the delivery sheet, please. Your tea will be in the kitchen when you have finished."

The driver says, "Any biscuits, Julia?"

"No, you cheeky devil, there isn't. You're lucky you're getting a cup of tea."

"Only joking, Julia; we will bring our own next time."

Julia asks, "How long will you be?"

The guard says, "About fifteen minutes."

"Okay, your tea will be on the tray in the kitchen."

"Cheers, Julia."

The driver says, "She is a little diamond."

"Yes, she is a good girl, all right."

Back on the street...

"I can't believe how slack it is, Jack. The procedure looks too easy. Surely we must have missed something."

"Well, we have seen it with our own eyes. The only thing I can imagine is that they treat it like scrap paper, and it's been going on for years without any trouble! So they have got complacent, and the fact it's around the back of the bank makes it less conspicuous as well."

"Oh, I don't fucking know, but whatever it is, it's an open invitation for a heist, don't you think?"

"I think you're right, Jack. I can't believe our luck. Now we need to hang around and see how long it is before the next delivery arrives and listen to see if the password is the same."

After hanging around all morning, it becomes apparent that the armoured trucks arrive every one and a half hours, and the password stays the same. In the taxi travelling back to Euston, the conversation is being kept down to a whisper. Loose lips sink ships, etc.

"Well, what do you think, Frank? It's just a matter of time before somebody does it, so why shouldn't it be us?"

"I see your point, Jack. I must say it looks enticing. It looks too easy, well, based on what we have seen today. I think it's worth taking it a bit further; it can't do any harm, I suppose. We have got to look at all the angles in fine detail and plan as best we can. It's like when we assess a new building contract, it always turns out more complicated than it looks at first glance. It can't be that easy, or one of the East End gangs would have done it, surely to God."

They arrive at Euston and get back on the train. In typical fashion, they go straight into first-class, of course.

"Do you fancy a beer, Jack?" It seemed like a silly question to ask.

"Why not? I think we have earned one after a hard day at the building exhibition."

Once in the buffet car, Frank says, "Two lagers, please, barman."

The barman, with a strong Birmingham accent, says, "Certainly, sir." He serves the drinks. "That will be seven pounds twenty, please, sir. Have you had a good day in the city, gentlemen, with plenty of cut and thrust, wheeling and dealing, that sort of thing?"

Jack says, "Well, yes, you could say we have been putting together a little business plan that should make us quite a bit of money if we go ahead with it."

The barman says, "You guys amaze me; you seem to thrive on risk."

Jack says, "Well, you could say that, but this one is as safe as money in the bank, isn't it, Frank?" Frank smiles.

The barman says, "I have heard that a few times on this train. Give me the easy life; I don't need the stress, thank you very much."

Jack says, "Cheers, mate."

The barman says, "Cheers, both. I hope your plan works out okay."

Back at the office on Friday morning, more aggravation builds up. Poor Karen is taking a lot of flak.

Jack asks, "Any problems while we were in London yesterday, Karen?"

"Nothing much apart from the bailiffs asking on the phone what had happened to the arrears payment for the council tax."

"Phone them back and tell them we have introduced a new system. Tell them that we put all the names of our more serious debts in a hard hat, and we draw three out each week and pay them. You can tell them that if they don't stop phoning us, they won't be going in the hat next week."

Karen answers, "You can't be bloody serious, can you, Jack?"

"Karen, if I took everything that's happening seriously, I would have bloody well hung myself by now," Jack says, raising his voice. "If I have learnt one thing in this life, it is, don't let the BASTARDS grind you down! Just remember that, Karen!" Jack shouted.

Karen goes quiet for a few seconds and looks out of the window, turns back and says, "Yes, of course you are right, Jack. I will keep that in mind when I get shitty phone calls in the future."

Jack realises he has upset Karen by shouting at her.

Jack says, "Sorry, sweetheart. I didn't mean to shout. It just makes me so angry when I think of what these bastards at the bank are putting us all through. They are destroying the business that Frank and I have taken years to build, with blood, sweat, and tears, and not much else. But that's not your worry; you are doing everything you can, and I hope you know we both appreciate it. But you mustn't let them get you down, or they have won, and we are not having that, are we, girl?"

"No, we are not having that, Jack. I know what you are both going through. It must be hell. Let me put the kettle on and make us a nice cup of tea."

"That's the best thing I have heard all morning. Nice one, Karen."

It's now Saturday morning. Jack arrives at the office in his Jag and hides it around the back of the barn. Frank arrives five minutes later and does the same. Both look around for bailiffs as they walk towards their grand-looking offices, which they designed and built themselves in the style of a country manor, set in its own grounds.

Picture of the Offices

Jack opens the door for Frank.

"I don't know about you, Jack, but I am sick of feeling like we are trespassing when we come here. We are being treated like common fucking criminals."

"I know what you mean, Frank. It isn't fair, and that is why we should hit back. They're treating us like criminals, so we might as well become fucking criminals. I don't know about you, but I am becoming quite obsessed with the idea of robbing a bank. I can't think of anything else. Wendy thinks I have got another woman. It's a good job she doesn't know the other woman is a bank in Islington, Frank."

Both laugh as they walk into the boardroom.

"I know, Jack, I feel the same. It's keeping me awake at night just thinking about it; it keeps going over and over in my head. Do you really think we could get away with it?"

"Well, let's have a look at it. The best thing we can do is treat it as a new venture, financed by the bank without us having to ask them."

"Instead, we will tell the wankers, I mean bankers, although on second thoughts, they should put 'W' where the 'B' is. That would be more in line with the Trade Descriptions Act, don't you think?"

They both laugh.

"That definitely sounds like a fair description to me. Right, it's a waste of time talking about the business; that would be called flogging a dead horse. Let's sit down and work our way through the plan and see if we think it would be possible to do it and, more importantly, get away with it. At least it will take our minds off all this shit."

Jack slams his hand down on a pile of final demands on the boardroom table.

"Well, Frank, the first thing is to set the date and work back from there. I think a Thursday would be best because that's the day we checked the place out, and we know the routine; it might be different on other days."

"Yes, you're right, Jack, but which Thursday? How long do you think we need to get everything sorted?"

"Pass me the diary, Jack. How about three weeks next Thursday? How does that sound? That gives us almost a month; what do you think?"

"It sounds long enough to me. What date is that?"

"It's 28 June. That suits me. I haven't got anything planned. How about you, Jack?"

"I don't think either of us will have anything to do by then the way things are going. Don't write anything down: no clues, no convictions. That's got to be paramount if this is going to stand any chance of working, Frank."

"Of course I won't, you arse. What do you think I would put in the diary? Out all day doing a bank robbery? Give me a bit of credit."

"No need to take the piss, Jack. Like Lord Nelson said, 'Loose lips sink ships.' Right, the next thing is modus operandi."

"You and your big words. What the fuck is that supposed to mean?"

"It means the plan and how we execute it."

"Well, why the fuck didn't you say so?" Jack says.

"It's Latin, you ignorant bugger. Didn't you know that?"

"No, I bloody well didn't know that, smart arse. So, let's stick to English, shall we? This is the London job, not the fucking Italian job. Well, anyway, this is how I see it: we hire a narrowboat from Brinklow Wharf—"

Frank butts in, "Wait a minute, did you say a bloody narrowboat? What the bloody hell are you talking about? I thought we were trying to rob a bank, not go cruising on the Grand Union Canal."

"We are robbing a bank, Frank; calm down and listen to me. We need a way of getting the money out of London and getting it back here."

"You are trying to tell me that our getaway vehicle does four miles an hour tops?"

"Yes, and I will tell you why. As you know, Wendy and I have walked the canals for over twenty years, and we have never once seen a copper. Train stations, coach stations, airports—they are all crawling with them. But not the good old Grand Union."

"Well, yes, I can see what you mean now you mention it. I've never seen any sign of police when I went on that canal boat holiday with Mary a few years ago."

"Let me finish, Frank. Me and Wendy will take the narrowboat to London, mooring at Camden Lock. We get there on Wednesday, the 27th. You come to London on the early train on the 28th with the bags and the guns."

"What fucking guns? I don't like the sound of this at all. We haven't mentioned anything about guns before. Are you sure about this? I hadn't even thought about guns."

"Well, how the hell do you think we can rob a bank without guns? Don't worry, nobody will get hurt. We will use sawn-off shotguns with blank cartridges. Stop worrying, it will be okay, you will see."

"And precisely where is the sawn-off shotgun shop, or do we get them out of the Argos catalogue or maybe Amazon? They seem to sell every bloody thing nowadays."

"Don't take the piss, Frank; leave that one to me. I have some good friends in the farming community who need a few quid. They will sort some guns out for us. The farmers are feeling the pinch just like the builders. The banks aren't treating them much better than us. Just leave it with me."

"Okay, Jack, you seem to have the gun thing sorted. Mind you, it will have to be a few quid the way we are fixed now."

"Shut up, Frank, and listen. I am losing my drift. Right, on the Thursday, I'm in Camden, and you're in Euston. I have told Wendy I am going to visit the War Museum, knowing she won't want to come with me; she hates that sort of thing. Me and you both get taxis and meet in the next street down from the bank. We meet at 9:30 am precisely, no slip-ups; we change into our disguises and put the shooters in our jackets."

Frank shouts, "Shooters, bloody shooters! You have been watching too many gangster films. This isn't a bloody game; it's deadly serious."

"Shut up and let me finish. As I was saying, we go to the back of the bank dressed as 'workmen' working on the phone box just up the road from the bank. And when the first armoured truck arrives at 10:15 am, we will get the password by listening to the guard."

"And how are we going to perform that little miracle if we are up the road fixing the bloody phone box?"

"Using a hearing device, Frank, that's how. Don't you remember we talked about it when we were casing the bank?"

"Oh, yes, so we did mention something about that. I forgot all about it."

"Well, don't ever forget anything to do with this job if it's going to stand any chance of succeeding. We must always be razor-sharp on all the angles."

"Hang on a second, Jack, before you start dishing out the bollockings. We haven't even decided if we are really going to go through with it or not. But you are right, if we do commit to doing it, we have got to be hungry, like the old days. If we do go through with it, we can't afford any balls-ups, or else…"

"Don't even think of the 'or else', Frank; we have to stay focused at all times, even if we are just planning it."

"Sorry, Jack, the listening device is a good idea. I will start researching it. Don't worry, I won't let you down. If we do this, we are really in the last chance saloon; failing is not an option."

"Good lad. Right then, getting back to the plan: we go in thirty minutes before the second delivery. We will put a sign by the intercom saying, 'Fire drill in progress; put the 11:15 delivery back 30 minutes. Sorry for the inconvenience'."

"Good idea, Frank; that will give us a better chance of getting out of there. Then what?"

"When the girl lets us in, you grab her and put your gun to her head. Then I will kick open the door from the kitchen into the sorting area, and in the best cockney accent I can muster, I will shout, 'This is a robbery! Everybody keep calm and nobody will get hurt! Is that fucking clear?"

"I like it, Jack, and the cockney accent is a touch of genius, sending the cops down a completely different line of enquiry."

"Then I will tell everyone to get down on the floor, all except the manager and his assistant. I will threaten them and get them to lead me to the good twenties, and then get those two arseholes to load the cases double quick."

"But, Jack, what about the getaway? They will press the alarm button as soon as we leave."

"Way ahead of you, Frank. The girl you are holding will be our hostage; you will take her to the kitchen. I will tell the manager and all the employees that I have a police radio scanner, pointing to the listening device, and then I will say, if I hear of any reports of a 'bank robbery' in Islington for at least one hour after we leave, we will kill the girl and that they will be pulling the trigger by sounding the alarm. And make no fucking mistake, we will do it."

"But, Jack, we can't drag a girl across London with us; that would be crazy."

"No, but here is the clever part: we don't."

"So, what the hell are we going to do with her then?"

"We will gag her and restrain her using gaffer tape, then we will put her in one of those dumpster bins that were at the back of the bank, in the yard. Then when we are safely away, we will call the bank on a throwaway phone and tell them where she is. There is no way she will get hurt, and she will be our ticket out of there."

"And then what, Jack? You have got my attention now; this is getting exciting."

"The two of us will head for the boat by taxi, to load up the cases of cash. I will need a hand getting them there. Once they are safely stowed on board and hidden out of sight of my missus, you can then get a taxi back to Euston and get the train home and go straight to our local and have a few drinks; make sure you speak to plenty of people just in case you need an alibi. Just a belt-and-braces exercise detail, Frank. Then I will go to the World's End Pub, where I have arranged to meet Wendy for lunch after supposedly coming back from the War Museum."

"Well, Jack, I must admit, I am impressed you have really thought this through. I have got to give you credit; it all sounds possible. I will give you that."

"Thanks, Frank, you are the only fucker that will give me credit right now." They both laugh.

"All joking aside, Jack, if we are going to go ahead with this crazy idea of yours, we had better get on with the list of things to do. Time is on the wing."

"Yes, Frank, and that's where we will be heading if we pull this off. On the wing to sun, sea, and satisfaction. First class, of course."

"Of course, Jack, how else would a couple of successful bank robbers travel? Stop dreaming and get on with it. Let's start by making a full list of things to do. There is a lot to do before we can even think about flying anywhere."

Frank and Jack sit down and go over everything. They make a comprehensive list of everything they need to prepare for the big day.

"Frank, so I think we have just about talked ourselves into doing this, haven't we?"

"Yes, Jack, I think we have. Let's fucking do it! Okay, Jack, you take care of getting the narrowboat and the shotguns and get that old Bob Hoskins film *The Long Good Friday*; that was all East End talk in that film. We need to practise until it comes naturally. We need to come across as Cockney villains; that should give the cops a nice false trail to follow. I will get the listening device and book the train, paid in cash, of course; no clues, no convictions, eh, Jack? I will get the disguises, and you get the boiler suits with the BT colours and the cases. How does that sound, Jack?"

"It sounds like you are committed, Frank; that's how it sounds to me. Thanks, mate; it will work, I am sure of it. We are sharp; we have had to be all these years. We will have our clandestine meeting next Thursday night, and we will see how we have got on with the list. Let's say, seven o'clock at the office?"

"Okay, Jack, Thursday it is. We might need to speak in private through the week. We are going to need a code word for a private chat if we are with people. What about Wasp, seeing as we intend to sting the bank?"

"Not a bad thought, Frank, but Wasp isn't an easy word to slip into a conversation just like that. Let's just say, 'The Other Job'; that's much easier given our line of work. What do you think?"

"Good choice, Jack. 'The Other Job' it is from now on."

Jack and Frank leave for home.

Jack arrives home, parks the car on the drive and goes in. Wendy walks to greet Jack and helps him take off his coat.

"Well, have you had a good meeting with Frank? Did you have plenty to talk about?"

"I suppose you could say that; it was fairly constructive considering the state of affairs the company is in at the moment. What's for dinner?"

"Your favourite 'Chateau Briand', and I got you a nice bottle of wine to go with it."

"Wendy, I don't deserve you. All these years and you still spoil me; you are one in a million, you really are! Come here, let me give you a kiss. Now I don't want you worrying. Me and Frank have always found a way out of trouble in the past, and we will do it again. If the firm goes down, we will find something to take its place."

"I know, Jack, but you must admit it's scary at our age to think we could be left with nothing to show after all these years."

"I know, darlin', but we will see what happens. They can't keep a good man down. You know better than anybody else that I am a survivor."

"Yes, I do, and that is why I married mad Jack Redman. I will get the dinner ready; it will be about an hour. Is that all right?"

"Yes, of course. I have got to make a couple of calls; I will be in the study. Give me a shout when it's ready."

Jack goes into his home office and phones Neil, his dairy farmer friend.

"Hi, Neil, it's Jack Redman. How's it going, mate?"

"Bloody hell, Jack Redman. Well, if you want the truth, Jack, everything will be going soon if things don't soon pick up. I have been farming all my life, and I have never known it so bad! What with the state of the country and the supermarkets wanting the milk for next to nothing. Sorry, Jack, I have heard you and Frank are going through hell with the bloody banks. What can I do for you? I will help you the best I can as long as it doesn't involve spending money."

"No, Neil, I understand everybody is in the same boat. It isn't nice, is it? But we will survive; we always have, and we always will somehow, mate. Anyway, enough doom and gloom. Me and a friend of mine have been offered a bit of shooting up in Scotland, which I quite fancy. We need a couple of cheap guns, but nothing fancy. We will probably only use them once."

"Sorry, mate, no can do. Although I do know a fella who was trying to sell a couple of twelve boars, he offered them to me. They are old guns, but he reckons they fire okay. I don't know if he has still got them. I will give him a call and ring you straight back."

"Cheers, Neil, you're a mate. If he has still got them, you do the deal; you will get them cheaper than I could. If you get them, I will come over on Friday night and pick them up. Oh, and by the way, Neil, no names, no pack drill; we haven't got licences."

"Don't worry, Jack, they have never been registered; they are just old farm guns."

"Great, Neil, let's hope he hasn't flogged them; I will talk to you in a couple of minutes."

A few minutes later, the phone rings, and Jack picks up the phone.

"You're in luck, mate; he still has them. He wants £250 for the pair. Do you want me to do the deal?"

"Yes, please, Neil, if you would, that would be a great help. I will come over to you on Friday night at about seven o'clock if that's all right, mate?"

"Okay, Jack, consider it done. I will see you on Friday; don't forget the cash."

"Of course, I will see you on Friday. Cheers!"

The next morning, Jack drives to the boatyard at Brinklow, about seven miles away, to book the narrowboat. He parks the car and walks across the bridge and down the steps to the towpath. He walks about a hundred yards and enters the boatyard, and finds the ramshackle booking office. He knocks on the door and walks in. There is a weathered-looking old man sitting at a desk, wearing an old duffel coat, an open-topped shirt with a neckerchief tied around his neck and a navy-style cap.

Jack says, "Good morning. I am Roy Wilson. I phoned about a booking about an hour ago. Are you Mr Walton?"

"Yes, I am Mr Walton, but you can call me Billy. We are a family firm; we don't use second names around here. Us Waltons have owned this boatyard for over a hundred years. My grandparents and my parents hauled coal and steel through both world wars, and then the bloody railway took over. That's what got us into the leisure business."

Jack interrupts, "And now you have got the best fleet on the canals."

"Yes, I remember your call. So what can I do for you this lovely morning?"

"Well, Billy, as I said on the phone, I would like to book one of your splendid boats for two weeks, from the 21st June until the 4th of July; American Independence Day, as it happens."

"Do you celebrate it, then?"

"Well, I might this year if all goes well."

"Bloody Yanks, they think they own the world. Coincidentally, it's the Yanks that have cancelled for the dates you want. And that means it's lucky for you because you will get the pride of the fleet, the Victory."

"Oh, that's why you didn't like my Independence Day remark, was it?"

"Yes, but they aren't the only ones cancelling. This has been the worst season we have had in the last 15 years; nobody has got any bloody money for holidays. The bloody banks have murdered this country, the irresponsible bastards."

"Well, Billy, I can't argue with that; they have done more damage than Hitler did, without a doubt. Well, is my little holiday going to be all right for those dates, then, Billy?"

"Yes, I have put you in the booking diary; the boat will be all ready on the 21st. We open at eight o'clock."

"What about payment, Billy? Sharpen your pencil; I am not a rich man."

"Would it be cash we are talking about or that silly plastic stuff everybody seems so fond of nowadays?"

"Yes, of course, cash, providing the price is keen. None of that silly VAT lark."

"Was that cash with a receipt or good old-fashioned money?"

"Without suits me. I don't want you giving Her Majesty the pleasure of my money until you have given it a good rinse through your kidneys in that pub up on the bridge."

Billy smiles.

"You have got that right, Roy; you're a man after my own heart. I'll tell you what, let's call it a grand in the hand on the day you pick her up. How does that sound?"

"That sounds good to me, Billy. I will see you on the 21st."

"Okay, I will be here, God willing."

Jack leaves the office, walks along the towpath to his car and drives to his office.

Frank has sourced the listening device on the internet and arranged next-morning delivery at an empty house a couple of doors from his house. It has a false name on the parcel. The next morning, Frank is sitting on a chair in his bay window, looking for the delivery guy.

He sees the guy looking bewildered as he knocks on the door of the empty house. Frank goes out and shouts, "Is that parcel for me? I am expecting one this morning."

The delivery guy walks towards Frank and says, "What name is it, sir?"

"Mr J. H. Green, 29 Laburnum Grove."

"Sorry, sir, it has got 25 on the parcel. Some stupid kid in our computer department, I expect; we get it all the time. It drives me mad. Well, I guess it's all sent to try us. Sorry about that, sir. Could you print and sign here, please?"

Thursday evening at the office, as arranged on Saturday, Frank and Jack arrive and go into the boardroom. They sit down, open their briefcases and take out their notepads, getting more and more enthusiastic with this great distraction from their crumbling business.

"Well, how have you got on, Frank? Have you made any progress?"

"Yes, it's going pretty well so far. I've got the listening device, and I have tested it. I can hear everything that's going on in the house across the road from my house. I always thought they got on until now; that has been an eye-opener. I have bought my return ticket to Euston for the 28th, and I got a good price by booking in advance. I paid cash, of course; no clues no convictions, eh, Jack?"

"Well done. I just pray that you use the return half of your ticket. I have managed to get the narrowboat for the dates we planned for, and I got it for a steal. The old boy who owns the boatyard is proper old school just like us. I really hit it off with him; the very mention of cash made his ears shoot up like a jackrabbit. A great guy, a real rough diamond; we need more like him, not like these wankers today, born with a calculator in one hand, a mobile phone in the other and a mouse up their arses." They both laugh.

Frank says, "It's really coming together now. We are really getting organised; it's like starting a new site. How about the guns? Have you had any luck with locating them?"

"It's all organised. I am picking them up tomorrow night from an old farmer mate of mine. You have met him, Neil from Holt Farm. I told him that we had been invited to Scotland to do a bit of rough shooting. The guns are perfect; they have never been registered, and they are just old farm guns. And only two hundred and fifty pounds for the pair, lucky or what?"

After finishing making new lists, they adjourned the meeting until the next Saturday morning and went to the Bull for a couple of pints.

It's Friday night, and Jack sets off for Holt Farm in his beloved Jag. He makes his way up the bumpy farm road, cursing every bump as he goes. He parks the Jag, walks to the farmhouse door, and knocks on the door. Neil opens it.

"Jack, you old bugger, come in."

"I can't believe how rough that bloody road of yours is; it would give a tractor a bloody good workout, let alone my poor Jag. Well, how's tricks, Neil?"

"Tricks is about right, Jack. The trick is keeping the farm running, what with this bastard recession. I've never known anything like this. I don't know which way to turn, and that's the truth."

"Well, knowing a canny old fucker like you, you should start by turning your mattress over."

"You cheeky bugger, everybody thinks farmers have got money hidden away just because we deal in cash a lot."

"Well, they should have; they find it very difficult to part with any of it in my experience. I've never met a starving farmer yet, and I don't think I ever will."

"Stop taking the piss. I can't remember the last time you bought me a pint."

"3rd April 2003 in The Crown at Napton; at twenty-two minutes past eight, as I remember it."

"Ha fucking ha! Always the joker, you don't change. Mind you, it wouldn't be you, would it? And you always have a way of making me laugh, and I haven't done that for a while."

Angie, Neil's wife, enters the room.

"Hello, Jack, I thought it was your laugh I could hear. We haven't seen you in a long time! What are you up to?"

"Up to is about right, Angie. I am up to my neck in it at the moment, but don't you worry about me. I am still ducking and diving, bobbing and weaving; you know what I am like. I will always pull a rabbit out of the hat when push comes to shove."

"Jack, you have been ducking and diving ever since we met you all those years ago. Well, a silly question, would you like a drink, Jack?"

Neil says, "That's like asking the Pope if he is Catholic, Angie. Of course, he would and so would I, but we will have one when we come back from the barn; we will do the business first. Business before pleasure, eh, Jack?"

"All right, I will pour you a couple of large whiskies and leave them in the parlour."

"You had better leave the bottle, Ange; me and Jack need a bit of cheering up."

"All right, love, but don't let Jack drink too much; he has got to drive home, remember."

"Come on, Jack, let's get the deal done, then we can have a drink, a chat, and a catch-up. It will be like old times. To be honest, it will be nice to have a conversation with somebody away from the village. Everybody I talk to around here is depressed, and it doesn't help when we are struggling like this."

"I know what you mean, Neil, but don't let the bastards get you down; we will get through this one way or another. I know we will."

Neil says, "Follow me, it's getting dark, so watch your step."

Jack steps in some cow shit.

"Fuck me, Neil, there's cow shit everywhere."

"Well, this is a dairy farm; the cows don't only make milk, they produce a fair amount of shit as well."

"I suppose you are right. I never really thought of that, being a townie. The only cows I have ever met wore short skirts, high heels, and lots of lipstick."

Neil bursts out laughing.

"You are a fucking lunatic. Here we are; this is your pair of Purdeys, Jack."

"Fucking hell, Neil, was the bloke you got these off called Oliver by any chance?"

"Oliver, no! What do you mean?"

"Oliver, second name Cromwell? Ring any bells?"

"You smart arse, do you want them or not? Don't fuck me about; I have gone to a lot of trouble to get these for you."

"Well, yes, I can see that it would take a lot of trouble to break into a museum after dark."

"Very funny, Jack, take it or leave it; £200 for two unregistered guns is a bargain. He wanted £250. I got you a good price. So do you want them or not?"

"Of course I will have them, just having a bit of fun, no offence meant, me old mate."

"All right, no offence taken. I am just a bit touchy the way things are, sorry, Jack. Let's put the guns in your car, give me the readies, and we will have that drink."

Jack puts the guns in the boot of the Jag and hands Neil the two hundred quid, and they both go back to the farm for a drink. After a lot of small talk and a fair amount of whisky, Jack leaves the farm under the light of a full moon.

Angie shouts, "Goodnight, Jack, come again soon; you have cheered Neil up no end. Oh, and bring Wendy with you next time?"

"I will, see you soon! Missing you already." Jack smiles and thinks, *One way or another, you won't be seeing much of me in the future.*

It's Monday night. Jack and Frank are in the boardroom, watching a DVD of *The Long Good Friday*, starring Bob

Hoskins as an East End gangster. They are practising their Cockney accents. Jack can't stop laughing, and Frank can't help laughing with him. Then Frank says, "Come on, Jack, let's get serious. It is bloody important that we sound like EastEnders. It's crucial that we give the cops a red herring. They wouldn't dream it's a couple of chancers from the Midlands who did it if we can get this bit right. We have only got two weeks to go; you are setting sail in a week. Time seems to be flying now, don't you think?"

"Yes, you're right, Frank; we have got to give it our best shot."

"Speaking of the best shot, did you get the guns?"

"Yes, they're in the boot of the car. I will go and get them."

Jack brings the guns in and shows Frank.

"Fuck me, these are out of the dark ages, Jack! Who sold them to you, Del Trotter? Whoever it was, they have got away with daylight bloody robbery by the look of these poxy things; they're not worth two hundred quid, nowhere near that. We couldn't walk in the bank with these bloody rusty things; they would laugh at us."

"Don't worry, they will look the part when we have adapted them in the workshop."

"I hope you're right, Jack; we can't go in with Mickey Mouse guns; they would rumble us straight away."

"Stop worrying. When we have done the business on them tomorrow night, they will look scary enough, trust me. And besides, who in their right mind would think the East End boys would go in with dodgy old guns? You look at it from their point of view, would you put it to the test? I know I wouldn't. Bollocks to that; why would they take the risk?"

"You're right, Jack, who would take the chance? I think we'll probably do something with them; we will see what they look like when we have done the work on them."

"I am sure they will be okay. When we have finished adapting them, we will do a thorough clean-up, and we will chuck all the bits we have taken off the guns in the old quarry. The water there is over 100 ft deep. We must keep our strict no clues policy going, no matter how much trouble it takes. It's got to be the perfect crime. I don't like the taste of porridge; how about you, Jack?"

"No, I don't like it either; it should never have got past the Scottish border, as far as I am concerned. Although I do like bars as long as they are the sort with sunshine and pretty girls behind them, serving exotic cocktails. That's the goal, Frank, not bars on cell windows; that's why this has got to be the most organised job ever planned by me and you. It doesn't matter how much it takes; it's got to work. This is our last chance; there's no other way out of all this shit."

"Jack, have you worked out the weight of 8 million in twenty-pound notes?"

"Yes, I weighed the grand that we have put aside for the narrowboat, and it will fit in four standard suitcases with wheels on. It's about twenty-five kilos in each case, a hundred kilos in the four. I have estimated that they will easily hold 8 million."

"Two each, that will be awkward, Jack, but I guess we will manage; they need to be good-quality cases with four wheels."

"Well, it's a good job you worked it out. It's all about detail; we don't want any surprises on the day, do we? By the way, I meant to ask you, how did Wendy react when you surprised her with the narrowboat holiday?"

"Well, the first thing she said, of course, was that we can't afford to be hiring boats and going cruising with the state the company is in at the moment. Then I explained to her that an old business friend of mine booked it and paid for it last year, and since then he has split up with his wife, so he let me take over the booking for four hundred quid, which is about a third of the real cost. I said it was too good to turn down, and besides, it's more than likely it will be the only chance we are going to get of a holiday this year or maybe for a few years to come; who knows what the future holds? Once she heard all that bullshit, she got quite excited about the idea. We have walked the canals for years, but we have never been on a narrowboat. I must admit I am quite looking forward to the trip to London myself. I just hope I get a chance to enjoy the journey back home."

"Yes, let's pray that you do. Well, that's good news that Wendy is okay with it. I thought you would have trouble convincing her. But I should have known that Jack the charmer would pull that little trick off without too much trouble. Well, I think that will do for today. Let's hide the guns in the workshop and fuck off to the pub for a swift one, my son."

"What you mean, Frank, is let's go down the frog and toad to the rubber dub for a pint of pig's ear."

"I know exactly what you mean, Cockney Jack; you will be telling me next that you are a Millwall supporter." They both laugh.

The next night, after dinner, Frank and Jack make their excuses and drive to the workshop to do the business on the guns. After a couple of hours, they have finished.

"Jesus, Jack, you were right; they look like something out of a gangster film; they really do! I can't believe how scary they look."

"I told you they would, ye of little faith. Now let's put all the bits in a bag with a couple of house bricks, hoover the place up, and leave things exactly as we found them. On the way to the pub, we will stop off at the old quarry and chuck the bag of bits over the cliff into the water, where it's over a hundred foot deep. That's the perfect place to dispose of the evidence; nobody would ever find it there. We must always stick to our no clues, no convictions policy."

"I like it, Jack. If we stick strictly to that formula and our detailed plan, it will work. We have got to show the pros that a couple of old builders, or should I say chancers, can do a more professional job than them. Listen to me, I am sounding like we can get away with it. God, I hope we can."

"Well, don't get carried away; we have got a long way to go yet, on a slow boat at that. I have had a thought, Frank; this will go down in history books as the bank robbery that went through the most locks."

"I never thought of that, Jack; we might go in the Guinness Book of Records."

"As long as we don't go down with criminal records, Frank, I don't give a fuck what we are in. I have got to say, with all that's going on, the business being in the shit and this job, it's getting to me a bit, trying to keep it all in my head. How about you?"

"Well, I think we have got to think of it like just another deal. So, if we pull it off, we celebrate like we always did, and if we don't, we have got free bed and board for the rest of our lives. As to the building business, it's as good as gone, so there's nothing we can do about that. So, let's just focus on the new deal and fuck the old ones."

They lock up the workshop and get into Frank's car. They head for the quarry to dispose of the parts they took off the guns. They drive up the quarry lane slowly; it's pitch black, and with the aid of a torch and the car headlight, Jack gets the bag out of the boot of the car. The place appears to be deserted. With one almighty effort, Jack hurls the bag over the quarry cliff, and they both hear a loud splash, followed by a loud cry from night fishermen.

"Who the fuck threw that? We are trying to catch fish down here!"

Jack and Frank run back to the car; they can't get their breath because they are laughing so much. They drive to the pub for a well-earned pint.

Our two chancers spend the rest of the week juggling the business and preparing for Jack's sail away and all the other bits, the tension rising daily.

It's the last Saturday before Jack sets sail for London. They meet at the office for a dress rehearsal, and to dot the i's and cross the t's on the fine detail for the job. Both put on the overalls, the false beards and the dark glasses. They pick up the guns and start talking to each other with Cockney accents, with, as you can imagine, lots of laughter.

Frank suddenly says, "Well, Jack, let's get serious; we look the part, we can talk the part, and we have planned every detail; we have just got to keep our heads and get on with it. At least that's the way I see it. How about you?"

"We have definitely passed the point of no return; this is our chance, Frank, and we have got to grab it with both hands and say goodbye to all the shit that our fucking bank is putting us through. It's in the lap of the gods and Lady Luck, and we need a lucky break. Fuck me, Frank, we deserve a bit of luck, don't we?"

"Whatever will be will be, sayeth the Lord."

"Well, as long as it isn't the Lord Chief Justice at the Old Bailey you're talking about, Frank."

"You can get that out of your head, mate. I wish I hadn't said that now, me and my big mouth."

"Don't be daft, Frank. We just need to give it all our concentration and thoughts to succeed with what we are about to do. And keep our bank in the back of our minds; that will spur us on to pull this off and get us out of all this crap that we are in now."

"You're not wrong there, Jack. We can't lose this; it's the only option we have got at this stage. Well, I had better get going. I have promised to take Mary out shopping this afternoon. So, I will see you on Monday morning. If you think of anything we have overlooked, give me a bell."

"Will do. See you on Monday. Cheers, Frank."

Frank is out shopping with his wife; they are sitting in the coffee shop at Sainsbury's. Mary says, "What's going on, Frank? You are miles away lately. You hardly talk to me. Is it the business problems that are getting you down?"

"Yes, it is. I am sorry, me and Jack are going through hell at the moment; it's a massive distraction. I don't like giving up, but I can't see any way out of this. Me and Jack are trying all the angles we can, but barring another bank coming on board, we are done for, I am afraid."

"Well, a trouble shared, Frank. Don't hold it in, or you will be ill, and that will only make things worse. When we first got married, we had nothing, and we were happy then, weren't we?"

"Yes, my darling, we were, weren't we? What would I do without you, my dear Mary? I am sorry, I just feel like I am letting everybody down. I promise not to be so distant in the future. You must be as worried as I am. It's daft, really. I keep going around and around in circles; it's like being in a room with no doors, but I can't stop looking for one."

"Well, it's not your fault, Frank; it's the bloody bank's fault, not yours or Jack's. You will find a door in that room one day; I know you will."

Mary kisses Frank on the cheek and says, "Drink your coffee, love; it's getting cold."

On Monday morning, Jack and Frank are in Frank's office going over and over everything again and again. It almost feels like they are rehearsing a play, but nobody would be clapping at this performance, that's for sure. Time seems to be flying now; they decide to have their final get-together on Wednesday evening.

It's now Wednesday evening. Frank and Jack are in the boardroom at the office.

Jack opens by saying, "Well, Frank, this is it. The adventure begins. I can't believe we have come this far, but we have, and it's too late to turn back now. We have got to stay strong and totally focused, and we will stand a good chance of getting away with it. What have we got to lose? The business is fucked, the bank has taken care of that. What a shower of shit they have turned out to be; just thinking about the duplicitous bastards gives me the determination to carry on. Frank, when we are doing the job, just keep thinking of the way we have been treated, and that will give us the courage and motivation to go through with this. This is payback time. I will ring you when I am on my way tomorrow morning just to let you know the plan is underway. If anything crops up, call me on my mobile; it will be on twenty-four seven."

"Don't worry, Jack, I will; but you ring me every day and give me a progress report. Especially on Wednesday from Camden. Well, bon voyage, as they say in France."

Frank shakes Jack's hand, looks him in the eye and says, "We can do this, old mate. We are a good team; we have always worked well together for all these years. You are like a brother to me; I wouldn't trust anybody else to take this risk with."

"Thanks, Frank, and you, mate, we have been to hell and back. All right, let's just hope we can get to London and back; that's what we need to do now. This seems like a dream; let's hope it doesn't turn into a fucking nightmare. Cheers, Frank. I will see you in Islington next week."

"Good luck, Jack; I will see you next week."

The next day at Jack's house, Wendy is dashing around, packing the last few bits and bobs in a carrier bag. Jack shouts, "Come on, old girl, we are going to be late."

Wendy shouts back, "What's the rush? It's not a plane we are catching; the boat won't go anywhere without us."

"No, I suppose you're right, but I just want to get underway, that's all."

Finally, Wendy and Jack get in the car and set off for the boatyard. They are just about to arrive, and Wendy says, "Are you sure you will be able to drive the boat? You have never done it before."

"Of course I will. You have seen some of the idiots that drive them when we have been out walking. If they can, I am sure I can; besides, old Billy Walton will show me the ropes. I am getting quite excited about getting to the bank."

"Don't you mean the boat?"

"Did I say bank? I meant to say boat. I was probably thinking of the canal bank. Well, here we are, and there's Billy. Good morning, Billy, is everything ready for us on the Victory, the pride of the fleet, as you described her?"

"More or less, let me get me cap. I can't go on board out of uniform; that would never do. Right, let's go. I will show you around her and give you a swift bit of tuition; she has been cleaned and filled with fuel, and she is ready to go."

"So where is the pride of the fleet, Billy?"

"More to the point, Roy, where is my grand in the hand we agreed on?"

"Here you are, you old bugger. I bet you never slept worrying about that."

"I slept like a baby thanks to the eight pints of Guinness I had for my supper. But I always feel better when the money is in my palm; you can't be too careful in these troubled times. I am not saying you look like a robber, Roy. Robber Roy, there's a joke there somewhere. I will have to give that some thought."

"Well, that's reassuring, Billy. I wouldn't like to think that anybody thought I looked like a robber."

Jack, Wendy, and Billy walk from the office and down the towpath towards the pride of the fleet, and there she is, the Victory. "I thought Billy was bullshitting, but she really is a fine-looking vessel."

Billy shows Jack around the craft, as he calls it, and takes him for a short journey down the canal as far as the turning point, and then he lets Jack drive it back, while Wendy makes herself busy down below, finding her way around the inside of the boat. They get back to the yard and moor up. Billy steps off the boat on to the towpath.

"Well, Roy, I am pleased to tell you that you have passed your driving test and that you are now officially the Captain of the Victory. Just be careful not to lose an eye and get your leg blown off, just my little joke, Roy. Oh, and if you break down, call the AA."

"The AA, Billy, really, the AA? I didn't know they did boats."

"No, just pulling your leg. The yard number is by the tiller, but you won't need it; she is as sound as a pound."

Wendy shouts from inside the boat, "If we break down near a pub, he won't mind."

"Now then, Wendy, Billy will get the impression that I will be driving the pride of the fleet under the influence of alcohol."

"Don't worry about that, Roy; there are no coppers on the canals; you needn't worry about drinking and driving boats. I have been doing it since I was a youngster."

"I hope you are right, Billy. Cheers, I will have her back in two weeks, all in one piece, God willing."

"I hope you have a good trip. You will soon get used to her. Think of her as a woman and handle her carefully and try and keep the water below your waist." Billy laughs as he waves them off.

"Jack, why does Bill keep calling you Roy?"

"Oh, that, I thought you were looking a bit bemused by that. The reason is quite simple. I didn't change the name on the original booking. I thought there might be a transfer charge. That was the name of the guy, the one I told you about that got divorced."

Jack sends Wendy to the front of the boat to cast off and shouts, "Hurry up, Wendy, you can move faster than that."

Wendy casts off and walks back towards Jack and steps on board. "What's the rush? We are supposed to be on holiday, aren't we? And you just remember what Billy told you: handle women carefully, and that means me as well as the bloody boat."

"No rush, sweetheart. I just want to get out of the yard so that we don't hold anybody up that are behind us; that's all it was. Sorry if I shouted. I am just a bit nervous with the boat and everything that's going on. I can't get my mind off the job. I will be all right once we get going."

"Jack, just calm down. If hold-ups happen, they happen."

"Many a true word spoken in jest, sweetheart, many a true word."

"And what the hell is that supposed to mean? You keep talking in riddles lately."

"Oh, nothing. Just thinking aloud. My mind is all over the place at the moment, what with the business and everything."

They set off. Jack is getting the feel of the boat, and Wendy is unpacking the cases and getting things organised in general. A couple of hours and two sets of tricky locks later,

Wendy surfaces with two large gin and tonics. "Here you are, Captain; this will put you in the holiday mood."

"Well done, Bosun, that will splice the mainbrace."

"What does that mean, Jack?"

"I haven't got a clue; I must have heard it somewhere. I think it's an old navy saying. I am sure Billy Walton could tell us. I will ask him when we get back. But you are right, my dear, plenty of fresh air and a nice G&T has got me feeling a lot better, thanks, sweetheart. What would I do without you?"

They moor up at about six o'clock outside a lovely looking gastropub called the Old Lock Gate, where they have a sumptuous meal and two bottles of a particularly fine Spanish Rioja.

Wendy and Jack are chatting about holidays they have had abroad over the years.

Wendy remarks, "Well, Jack, we have been lucky enough to see the world, but I suppose the Grand Union Canal will have to do for now. I can't see us going overseas again in the near future or the far distant future, for that matter."

"Never say die, Wendy; we might go abroad again. It just depends on how things turn out. You know me; I am a great believer in fate. If it's on the cards, it will happen."

"Oh, Jack, that's what I love about you. No matter what happens, you are always optimistic; you never give in, no matter what."

"Well, you know I like the glass half full, not half empty."

"You like the glass full, but it doesn't stay full for long when you're around. Come on, let's get to bed. I suppose you want to start our cruise early in the morning. But if you do get going early, leave me in bed. I will be dreaming I am on a sunny beach somewhere exotic."

"Okay, sweet dreams!"

Jack and Wendy have been travelling for three days, and all is going to plan until they come up behind two other boats waiting to go through the lock. The old, crotchety lockkeeper walks alongside.

Jack says, "Is everything all right, me old mate?"

"No, it's not all right; some bloody fool has gone too quick into the next lock down, run into the sluice gates, and jammed them so nothing can get through. I am afraid you will have to moor up for the rest of the day while they get it fixed. Pull over there and try not to hit the bank; it's a bit loose."

Jack thinks to himself, *Try not to hit the bank, you silly old fucker; that's exactly what I am trying to do. Fuck, I knew something like this would happen to put a spanner in the works.*

After mooring up, Jack goes inside to look for the chart to see exactly where he is and if he thinks he can still make it on time. He shouts to Wendy, "Where is the bloody canal chart? I need to see how far it is to London."

Wendy climbs down into the cabin. "Stop panicking; we are on holiday. There's no rush, is there? I put it away in the drawer."

"Which bloody drawer? This boat is full of bloody drawers."

"Well, they're not in my drawers; you seem to have lost your way to them on this holiday. You usually get quite frisky when we are away from home."

"Yes, you're right; I am. Let's see now." Jack draws the curtains, grabs hold of Wendy, lifts her up and lays her on the bed, and the old Jack pushes the passion button. And a steamy session begins after about an hour.

There is a knock on the window; it's the crotchety old lock keeper. "I don't like knocking while the boat's a rocking, but I thought you should know they have freed the gates at the next lock; you can get through now."

Jack shouts, "Thanks, mate, I was just sorting my tackle out."

The lock keeper walks away mumbling, "I thought that's what you were doing. I wish some bugger would sort mine out; it hasn't worked for years."

Back at the office, Karen takes the mail to Frank. "It looks like more doom and gloom, Frank, and there is one there from the dreaded bank."

"Yes, Karen, I suppose you're right; we don't get much fan mail these days. It's only a matter of time before the bastards go for the jugular. Karen, you have been great to put up with all this shit. But if you chucked it in now before the axe finally falls, me and Jack wouldn't blame you if you went and found another job. We would give you a glowing reference, you know that. I don't know about a reference; you deserve a bloody medal for bravery in the field." They both laugh.

"I know, Jack, but I couldn't leave you when you're in trouble; you have both been good to me over the years, and I am not going to abandon ship now. Talking of ships, I wonder how Jack and Wendy are getting on with their boating holiday. He will probably only get as far as the first pub; what do you think, Frank?"

"No, he wouldn't do that, Karen. He loves the canals too much. He will probably ring us from Venice next week; I wouldn't wonder." They both can't help smiling thinking of mad Jack and his past antics.

"Nothing would surprise me with that one; he is nutty enough to do anything. I'll go and make us a nice cuppa tea, and I have bought some of your favourite biscuits."

Frank thinks, *If only you knew, Karen, if only you knew how bloody nutty Jack really is; you wouldn't believe what he is up to right now even if I told you.*

As Karen leaves Frank's office, Pat, the Irish ground worker, brushes past her and bangs his hard hat on Frank's desk.

"Oh, and what seems to be your problem then? You nearly knocked Karen over the way you charged through that door."

"My problem, Frank, is that my last month's pay cheque has bounced; that's what my bloody problem is, and if I don't get some cash right now, I am fucking off, and I ain't coming back this time. I mean it, Frank; this is no joking matter. I have got a wife and six kids to feed."

"I am sorry, Pat, the cupboard is bare. I am very sorry. That's the way it is. You know the bank has stopped our line of credit; the two-faced bastards said they would help us, and they haven't. When I wrote your cheque, I had no idea they would bounce it; in fact, if you had banked it straight away, it would have gone through. It's just these last couple of days that they have frozen the account. The best I can offer is a good reference, Pat. I really am sorry."

Pat storms out of the office, walks across the yard to his pickup truck, and throws his Parker-Lake Homes hard hat at Frank's Range Rover. Luckily, it misses. He shouts, "Fuck you, Frank, you can stick your reference up your arse." He gets in his truck and speeds off.

In the meantime, Jack and Wendy are going through a lock, and Jack is showing signs of rushing.

Wendy says, "What's all the rush? I told you before, we are supposed to be on holiday. If you don't slow down, you will give yourself a heart attack."

"Sorry, sweetheart, I just don't want to be late getting into Camden Lock tomorrow. I don't want to miss my trip to the war museum the next day. I have wanted to go there for years, and for one reason or another, I have never got there. If we keep going at this speed, we should just make it in time. I am okay; I am still fit for my age."

"Well, I can't argue with that by the way you performed when we were waiting for the lock gate to be fixed. That was the young Jack Redman, and no mistake. Well, if you're that bothered about the dowdy old War Museum, carry on. I will make us a nice G&T."

That evening, after a nice meal on board and a few drinks, the boat got rocking again. After this stress relieving exercise, they retired for the night. The next morning, Jack didn't wake up until 8:30. He got dressed quickly and started the boat; it was going to be a long day if he was going to get to Camden Lock in time. He hardly stopped; he had his lunchtime sandwich while he was driving, and he didn't stop until it was nearly dark.

It's two o'clock the next day, and they are cruising into Camden Lock. Jack wipes his brow and thinks, *Thank fuck, we have made it in time. If we had been held up for the day at that bloody lock, we wouldn't have made it in time for the job.* Jack turns to Wendy and says, "Well, sweetheart, what do you think now that we are finally here? You can just imagine the characters that have been through here over the years."

"Well, there is certainly one coming through now, Jack Redman; they would have to go a long way to top you. Well, if you really want to know what I think, it's a canal with a lock with shops, pubs and restaurants from where I am looking. No, Jack, I don't think it was worth all the trouble. I think this is all about you going to the War Museum, that's what I think. We will take it a bit slower on the way back; we must have broken the record for getting from Brinklow to London by canal."

"Don't be daft, woman; you are in the heart of vibrant London, the capital city of our fair land. You will enjoy it when you go shopping tomorrow morning, while I am at the museum. And then for a special treat, we will meet up at the World's End, a great pub in the middle of Camden, and we will have a nice lunch and a drink. I will meet you there at two o'clock. Now let's moor up and have a large G&T. I think we deserve it; the sun must be over the yardarm somewhere in the world, and I promise we will take it easy going home."

"Jack, you are incorrigible; you will always find an excuse to have a drink. All right then, but you can make them. I am tired."

After a couple of G&Ts, they go for a walk around Camden, and Wendy starts to enjoy the vibrance of the place. She turns to Jack and says, "You were right, Jack; it was worth the trouble. This place is so lively, you can't help getting excited; it really is something. What do you fancy for dinner?"

"Well, if you're getting excited, I can think of something that's better than dinner."

"I think all this fresh air and getting away have turned you into a randy old man. Let's have dinner first, and we will see about getting the boat rocking later."

"Okay, that's fair enough, dinner first. Well, there is plenty of choice. How about a ruby?"

"A ruby? What the hell is a ruby?"

"A Ruby Murry is a Curry; it's a Cockney rhyming slang."

"Since when did you use Cockney rhyming slang?"

"When in Rome, do as the Romans do; it's just a bit of fun, Wendy. I looked it up before we left; it's quite interesting. The story goes that the Cockneys invented it so they could talk in pubs or any public place without the police knowing what they were talking about. I can see you're not impressed. Come on, let's find a nice Indian restaurant."

Jack asks a passer-by if he knows of a good Indian restaurant. The guy says in a northern accent, "No idea, mate. I am a milkman from Manchester."

Witty Frank retorts, "Fuck me, you've got a big round." They both laugh, and the northerner walks away.

After walking around, looking for a restaurant, they ask a cab driver for a recommendation. He says there's a great one in brick lane called Bengal Village. He offers to take them there for a tenner. They jump in the cab and are quickly taken to the restaurant. On the way, the cab driver says, "While you're down this way, you might like to have a drink in the Blind Beggar Pub; it was made famous by the Krays when they shot and killed George Cornell, a member of their rival gang, the Richardsons. It took place on 9th March 1966 in that very pub."

Jack says to the cab driver, "Thanks, we will have a drink in there after dinner. You certainly know your stuff. I am glad we asked you. I have heard you black cab drivers have to do the knowledge, but I didn't think it included knowing the history of London."

"Yes, Guv, we have to know all sorts in this job, but personally, it's the part of the job that I like the best. It's nice to help strangers to the capital enjoy the history of our great city. Well, I hope you enjoy your dinner. I don't think you will be disappointed. Goodnight, sir, madam." The cab drives off.

The cab driver was bang on; it is the best Indian food they had ever tasted, and to think they thought he only did it to get a fare. Jack and Wendy leave the restaurant and walk to the Blind Beggar Pub for a nightcap. As they walk in, they feel a macabre sense of going back in time. Jack orders a G&T for Wendy and a pint of best bitter for himself. He pays the barman, and they sit down. As they look around at the different characters, they fantasise about who they thought looked like villains. Jack thinks to himself, *I am probably the only villain in here, but Wendy doesn't know that, thank God.*

Wendy says, "Drink up, Jack; I don't like the feel of this place. Let's get back to the boat for an early night; you have got a big day tomorrow."

Jack thinks, *If only you knew how big, Wendy, like me, you wouldn't get much sleep tonight.*

They leave the Blind Beggar Pub and hail a cab. Twenty minutes later, they are back at the boat. Jack pours a large whisky and a G&T for Wendy. They both chat about the Indian restaurant and, in particular, the Blind Beggar Pub. Wendy says she felt uncomfortable in there.

"I kept looking around, half expecting gangsters to burst in with guns."

"That's funny you should say that, sweetheart. I was thinking about that sort of thing as well. I couldn't get it out of my mind."

After a restless night, Jack gets up at 6:30; he makes a cup of tea and sits on the side of the bed, his stomach churning contemplating the day ahead. He thinks, *What the fuck am I doing to this poor woman? She thinks I am going to the War Museum; instead, I am going out to commit armed robbery. And if it all goes tits up, she won't see me back here today. Come on, get a grip; that's negative thinking! I have got to be positive; it's got to work, or we really are fucked. Me and Frank have planned every detail; all we need now is the courage to go through with it and a bit of luck. God knows we deserve a bit of luck; luck seems to have deserted us lately.*

Wendy wakes up at 7:30 and says, "You were up early; couldn't you sleep? Was it the Ruby? Or did you have a nightmare about the Blind Beggar and gangsters bursting in with guns?"

Jack smiles. "It was probably something like that. I was tossing and turning all night, so when it got light, I got up to make a cup of tea. Can you do me a bacon sandwich and another cup of tea? I'll have that and get off to the War Museum nice and early to avoid the crowds. I think it's going to be a hectic day one way or another."

Jack finishes his bacon sandwich and a second cup of tea.

"Right, Wendy, I'm off. I will see you at two o'clock at the World's End Pub. Have a look at the street market…you will enjoy that. Don't spend too much." Jack kisses Wendy and turns to leave, but turns back and kisses her again. He says, "I do love you. I want you to know that no matter what we have to go through in the future, you do know that, Wendy, don't you?"

"Of course I know that, you daft thing. Now go and have a good time at the museum, although I can't see that it will be very exciting. All those weapons, tanks, and armoured vehicles. It's a men's thing. I can't see the fascination in things that could kill people. I don't think it will be exciting. I think you might be disappointed."

"Oh, I think it will have its moments. I will see you later at the pub, all being well."

"Go on, get off. Remember, you are in London; there could be hold-ups."

"Yes, you're right, sweetheart; there certainly could be. In fact, I am sure there will be at least one. See yah, later," says Jack while thinking, *I hope.*

Jack steps off the boat and walks along the towpath to hail a taxi; he looks at his watch, trips over a tether rope, and goes arse over head. He jumps up, feeling a right prat; he is quite shaken. He walks to the taxi, tells the driver where to go and gets in. He is thinking while they are driving through the busy London traffic. *What if I had broken my wrist or something when I fell? That would have fucked things up altogether. Well, I didn't, thank God. I will certainly thank God if we get away with this. I hope Frank is on time. We just need that bit of luck for this to work, and if it does, we are back on top. It seems strange that we were here in London just a couple of months ago, practically begging our bank to help us, and now we are back in London, not begging but demanding money. It's just a shame it's not a branch of our bank. I suppose that was too much to ask for. But they're all the bloody same; they are all in the shit and taking everybody down the toilet with them.*

Jack arrives at Bransbury Street, the street next to the rear of the bank. He pays the driver and tells him to keep the change. The taxi driver says "Thanks Guv"

Jack looks around and spots Frank across the road. *Thank God he is here early, as well as me.* He shouts across to him. Frank crosses the busy road. "Thank Christ you are here. I tried to phone you, and you didn't answer. I was thinking all sorts. Anyway, you are here now, good and early as well. Grab two of the cases...How are you feeling?"

"Bloody nervous, that's how I am. I have had a right game getting the four cases with the guns and disguises on the train and across London. My throat's gone dry. I could do with a drink; how about you? Daft question, your throat is always dry. Where could we get a drink around here at this time of day?"

"Very funny, Frank. Well, we have got forty minutes until we go into robbery mode. So, let's try and find somewhere to get a coffee, preferably an Irish one. That big hotel over the road looks decent, and we can change in the toilets. Come on, let's go. Jesus, look at the name: The Jury's Inn. What kind of name is that? I hope it's not some kind of warning?"

"Now then, Jack. You are getting paranoid; do you honestly think that a company named a hotel to warn us off? I don't think so somehow. Anyway, if the jury is in, we are okay. If the jury was out, that would be worse. If the buggers stay in, we are safe."

Frank and Jack cross the road, enter the hotel and walk into the coffee shop. Frank orders two Irish coffees. They are sitting drinking the coffee. They look at each other, both thinking in unison, *It's not too late to call this off.*

"Well, Frank, we are in the Jury's Inn, I am meeting Wendy in the World's End, and the bank is next door to the Robin's Hood Pub. So, what is all this telling us?"

"It's telling us, Jacky boy, that it's now or never…Come on, let's get changed in the toilets before we bottle it."

They look at each other, and bang, the adrenalin and the Irish coffee kick in. They both get up as if they were clockwork toys; they go into the toilets and change into their disguises. They come out one at a time, pick up two cases each and meet in the street.

"Right, Frank, the first truck is due in ten minutes; let's get in position." Their hearts are pounding. "Remember what we said: military precision, stay completely focused and we can do this. Remember everything we have rehearsed at the office, and we stand a bloody good chance of cracking this. Just keep thinking of the shit the bank has put us both through. Not just us, but our families as well, and that will get us through this; I am sure it will."

They walk into Florence Street and get near to the back of the bank, and then they hide in an alley. Jack fits the listening device on his head. Five minutes later, the first truck arrives right on time. Jack walks to the phone box, opens the door, and picks up the receiver. This is as near as he dare go without looking suspicious. The guard climbs out of the truck, goes to the intercom, and presses the button.

The guard says, "Good morning, Julie. It's the delivery; the password is Jackdaw."

"Okay, everything is ready for you; the pallets are on the bay. I will open the gates and put the kettle on."

"Thanks, darlin', you're too good to us."

The gates open, and the truck drives in. Jack walks back to Frank.

Frank eagerly asks, "Did you get it?"

"Yes, yes, I did. I can hardly believe it. If we ever needed a sign, the bloody password is Jackdaw. Out of all the birds it could have been, it's the bird that steals things! How bloody appropriate is that? It's got to be a sign; the stars must be aligned in our favour. Bloody Jackdaw! It's also my name, and I am going through the bank door; it's almost an invitation to steal the money."

Thirty minutes later, the armoured truck pulls out of the gates into Florence Street and drives off. Jack and Frank hide in the alleyway; twenty-five minutes to go.

Jack says, "Well, Frank, we will live or die today. Are you sure you still want to go through with this? Because you don't have to, even at this late stage, because if you don't, even though we have spent weeks planning it, not to mention a fair bit of money, if you really want to back out of it now, I will understand. After all, it was my idea. I will be pissed off with you, but I will respect your decision either way. So, is it a go, or is it a go home? It's your last chance to speak up. I say we do it. So, what do you say, Frank? He who dares and all that, bollocks. Well, what do you say? Come on, Frank, I need to know you are 100% committed to doing this, or it will go wrong, and we can't afford that to happen at any cost."

"Let's toss a coin, Jack; let's let the coin decide."

"Toss a coin! Toss a coin! I will toss you in a minute, over those fucking railings! You seriously want the rest of our lives to be decided on the spin of a fucking coin? Come on, Frank, be sensible; there is too much riding on this to be tossing fucking coins. This isn't some kind of game we are playing; this is real life. It doesn't get more serious than this. You know how important this is to both of us?"

"Yes, I do, but it's a test of luck. Don't you remember when we were in that casino in Marbella, and we put £500 on red and it won? We have always said, we need an element of luck. The spin will tell us whether luck is with us today or not."

"I can't believe what I am hearing. Like I said, that was a game, and we could afford to lose that game; we can't afford to lose this one. Okay, you old woman, here's a fifty pence piece; give it a good spin. I can't believe we are doing this. I really can't. We must be mad; that's all I can say. I think you are losing track of reality."

"Well, let's see what happens, Jack; you know how superstitious I am. I can't help it. My whole family is like this."

Frank spins the coin. Jack shouts heads. The coin spins in, and in what seems like slow motion, it lands on the floor, bounces, and finally comes to a stop.

Jack shouts, "Heads, it's bloody heads, and it's our dear queen's head! So I guess we have got her blessing to help ourselves to a banker's bonus, and why not? Well, Frank, you have got your sign now. Can we get on with what we came here to do?"

Frank says in a cockney accent, "Not arf my San, the dickery is ticking, so let's do it. The luck is telling us that we can do it. I am with you all the way now. That bloody coin and the password have convinced me that our luck is in."

"Yes, let's bloody do it, Frank; we will soon find out whether our luck is in or not."

Frank and Jack put on the dark glasses and leave the alley. They immediately go into typecast East End hard men. They walk towards the gates to face their destiny. The next thirty to forty minutes is about to change their lives for better or for worse. Jack puts the fire drill sign next to the intercom. With the adrenalin running at T max, he presses the intercom button and waits.

The intercom crackles, and a girl's voice asks, "Who is it?"

Jack says in his best Cockney accent, "It's the second delivery, darlin' Julie, isn't it?"

"Yes, it is, but you are a bit early. The lads haven't quite finished clearing the last load off the bay yet…You'll have to wait a bit while they finish clearing the bay."

Frank looks at Jack, wondering what to do. Jack has a gut reaction and pushes the intercom button and says, "Okay, Julie, but the lads down at the depot reckon you make a lovely cup of char. Any chance we could have one while we are waiting for the lads to finish clearing the bay? We haven't had a chance to have one this morning; we're both parched. There's a good girl."

"Oh, you guards are always getting me to make tea. I will have to start charging for it. All right, I will open the gates. Oh, silly me, what's the password today?"

"Sorry, darlin', I should have said it's Jackdaw."

"Okay, I will open the gates; knock on the door, and I will let you in for your tea."

Jack pushes the intercom button and says, "Thanks, darlin', you're an angel."

Frank says, "Well done, Jack, that was bloody quick thinking. Maybe the luck is with us. Come on, let's go; this is it! We must keep our nerve now, and we can do it. This can change both our lives forever if we get it right, so let's think of the banks and give them hell just like they have given it to us."

The gates swing open, and they walk down the yard to the side door, both shitting themselves, but it's too late to turn back now; they have reached the point of no return. They pull the guns out of their overalls and knock on the door. The girl opens the door and steps out.

"You're not the reg—" she tries to say, when Frank grabs her, puts his hand over her mouth, and gets her in a tight grip, putting the gun to her head.

He says, "Don't struggle and you won't get hurt. This is a robbery, but if you don't struggle, you will be all right. If you do struggle, so help me, I will blow your fucking head off. I mean it, so behave and you will live. Do you understand?"

The girl nods her head.

Jack bursts through the double doors, followed by Frank and the petrified Julie. Jack shouts in his best East End accent, "This is a fucking robbery! If anybody makes a move or pushes any alarm buttons, the girl is history, and so will be some of you. So be fucking sensible and nobody will get hurt. Do you fucking well understand me? Now everybody lay on the floor face down, all except the manager and his assistant. Right, Manager, what's you and your mate's name? Come on, speak up, you asshole."

With a trembling voice, he says, "We are both called Richard, but we call him Dick to save confusion. He is my assistant manager."

"Sounds about right to me, a pair of Dicks. Well, if you two wankers don't fill these suitcases with good twenties in ten minutes, you will be dead Dicks, and don't try any smartarse tricks, or Julie will get it. And I am not fucking joking." Jack looks at his watch and says, "You have got nine minutes and forty seconds left, so move or you will see a bloodbath and you two tossers will have caused it."

The manager and his assistant start furiously packing bundles of twenties into the suitcases. The manager shouts, "Everybody do as you are told; they can have the money. I don't want anybody getting hurt. Do exactly as you're told."

Jack shouts, "Faster, you bastards; the clock is ticking."

The manager, Richard, says, "Okay, okay, we are doing our best. Please don't kill us; we have done nothing wrong. Please, we have got families at home. We don't want anything to happen to any of us."

"Well, if nobody does anything silly, nobody will get topped. Do you fucking well understand me? This is 'YOUR FINAL DEMAND'!"

Frank shouts, "Faster, you pair of tossers, or I will waste the girl, and I can assure you she will get it, and so will you two."

All the staff are laying down in complete silence. When they hear a police siren coming towards the bank, the staff look at each other, wondering what the hell will happen next. Will these gangsters shoot their way out?

Frank and Jack struggle to control their bowels, thinking, *That's it; the game is up.* Then the siren starts to fade away; it has got nothing to do with the bank. Two minutes later, the suitcases are full and locked. The two managers step back, and Richard says, "Now you have got what you came for, and we have cooperated and done everything you have asked of us, so will you please leave the building?"

Jack shouts, "Right, now listen to me carefully! You two take the cases into the yard. My partner will go with you, and then you come back in and lay on the floor facedown with the others. We are taking Julie with us. We want one hour before you raise the alarm. If we hear any conversations about a bank job in Islington on our police scanner (he points to the listening device on his head), that will mean you have signed young Julie's death warrant. Make no mistake; we will shoot her in cold blood, and it will be you that will have pulled the trigger, do you all understand? This is a life-or-death situation you are all in, so don't fuck it up, or you won't ever see Julie again."

Frank reverses out through the double doors, dragging the girl with him. Jack does the same and shouts as he goes, "Remember what I said: don't do anything silly and the girl will live, do you hear me? Has it sunk in? Do nothing for one hour."

Richard the manager shouts, "Yes, yes, we understand; please go! Wait a second, where will you leave Julie? How will we know if she is safe?"

"We will phone the bank and tell you. Now just behave and do as you're told, and we will spare the girl. You have my word on it. Just don't panic and do anything silly and Julie will come back to you."

Jack slams the door and leaves. He takes the gaffer tape out of his pocket and gags the girl and binds her wrists and ankles together.

Then they lift her into an empty industrial bin.

Frank says to her, "Now stay calm and you will be all right. We will ring the bank and tell them where you are. Don't roll around or make any noise; we are putting an explosive device under the bin. It will automatically disarm in 45 minutes. Do exactly as you are told, and you will be perfectly safe. We are not bad bastards; we are not out to kill anybody. Do you understand?" Julie nods her head. "Good girl. You will be fine, I promise."

Jack and Frank put the guns in their overalls, grab the suitcases and walk up the yard. They press the button, the gates open and out they go into the street. Walking at a steady pace, hearts pounding, dying to run into busy upper street. After what seems like forever, they walk into upper street and mingle amongst the people on this busy thoroughfare.

Frank and Jack slip into a public toilet and change into their regular clothes. They put the guns, disguises and overalls into the backpack that Frank was wearing under his overalls. Jack pulls a small can of spray paint out of the backpack and quickly sprays the silver cases matte black.

They leave the toilet separately and walk down Pentonville Road, where they hail a black cab. They load the cases into the cab. Sticking strictly to their plan, they are going to change cabs in Finsbury. They leave the cab in Finsbury High Street and walk pulling the cases as they go.

Frank says, "That was a good idea of yours, Jack, not going straight to the boat."

Jack smiles and says, "I don't think we will ever go straight again, Frank."

They are walking down a busy London street, pulling God knows how much money along in the suitcases. Jack and Frank keep looking at each other in disbelief of what they have just done; it's totally surreal.

Jack says, "We had better ring the bank on the old Motorola phone; it's been nearly an hour."

"Yes, Jack, do it now while we are walking; those poor buggers are laying there thinking we have got the girl, and we might kill her."

Jack rings the bank.

A gay sounding voice comes on, "Yes, sir, my name is Jerome. How may I help you today?"

Jack says with a wry grin, "You can't; we have already helped ourselves. Now listen to me, this isn't a hoax call. You need to get in touch with Richard in the money sorting department at the back of the bank and tell him that Julie is in the big waste bin outside the back door in the yard. Have you got that? Oh, and thank him for his cooperation and his donation. And then ring the police. Do you understand me?"

"Ring the police? Whatever for, sir? Why would I do that?"

"Because, you fucking arsehole, the bank has been robbed, and that's who you ring when banks get robbed, you tosser. Now get on with it." Jack hangs up and puts the phone in his pocket to be disposed of later. "No wonder the banks are in the shit with witless wimps like that working for them. Well, that's a good job done. I would love to see the faces of those two Dicks when they find out that Julie has been in the bin all the time and the explosive device is an old house brick. They will feel so choked when they find out that they could have sounded the alarm the minute we walked out of the bank."

"So would I, Jack. They will get some stick from the cops when they get there. How easy was that, I can't believe it! What do the Americans say? It was like taking candy from a baby. There wasn't a man amongst them; they were all wimps. Mind you, it's a good job they were; it made our job easy. It would only have taken one lunatic who wanted to be a hero, and that would have fucked things up good and proper."

Frank hails a cab.

The cab driver says, "Morning, gentlemen, do you need a hand with those cases?"

Jack says, "No, thanks, they have only got a few pounds in them; we can manage, thanks." Frank smiles at Jack.

"Well, gents, where can I take you on this lovely sunny day?"

Frank says, "Camden High Street, please, cabby, and you are right; it is a lovely day."

They soon arrive in Camden High Street. They pay the cab driver, get the cases and start walking to the boat. They are walking down the sloping road into Camden Lock when Jack takes a deep breath and says, "I don't fucking believe it; there is a copper walking straight towards us. Don't panic, Frank. I will handle it. He is only an ordinary bobby on the beat; there's no reason why he should see us as suspicious."

The policeman says, "Good afternoon, chaps. You must be hot pulling those heavy cases. I think this is the hottest day we have had this year."

Jack says, "Yes, we are a bit hot, but we are going to put our cases on the boat, and then we are going to have a nice cold beer over at the pub before we cast off."

"You're lucky, I have got another six hours before I can have one."

"Oh, well, it will taste all that much better for the wait, don't you think?"

"I suppose you're right. See you again, chaps; you have made me thirsty talking about cold beer." He walks on.

Frank says quietly, "Not if we can fucking help it." They walk to the Victory and stow the cases on board in the front bunker and lock the door. They both sit down, mentally exhausted. Jack says, "Fuck the beer; I need a large scotch. How about you, Frank? Could you use a spot of nerve tonic?"

"I don't know about a large one, Jack. I think I could drink a bottle. I was shitting myself when you were talking to that bloody copper."

"So was I, but I knew I couldn't panic. Can you imagine we were standing within inches of a copper with millions in stolen money? Fuck me, Frank, what a day!" Jack pours two very large scotches, picks up his glass and hands one to Frank. "Cheers, mate, here's to health, wealth, and freedom. We are not out of the woods yet, but so far so good, Frank."

"Cheers, mate. Well, I had better head back to Euston and get my train home. It's twenty to two, Jack, you had better get your skates on; you have got to meet Wendy at the pub at two o'clock; you will be late."

"Hell, is that the time? Well, I might be a few minutes late, but when I left here this morning, I didn't know if I would get back at all. Come on, Frank, drink up, and let's piss off." Frank puts the backpack on with the guns and disguises in. They both stand on the towpath. Jack locks the boat up and walks with Frank to the main road. Frank hails a cab. They shake hands. Jack says, "Watch how you go, mate. Give me a bell and let me know how things are going and if you get back all right."

Then he adds, "And, Frank, make sure you burn everything down at your allotment and chuck the guns in the old quarry at night, and try not to frighten the fishermen this time. Oh, and take the flip phone, that can go in the bag with the guns."

The cab pulls up. Frank says, "Will do, Jack. See you in a week now. Get going, you will be late meeting Wendy."

The cab drives off. Jack turns and heads for the World's End Pub to meet Wendy. He is feeling very nervous now that Frank has left him on his own. The realisation of what they have done is just starting to sink in. Then he pulls himself together. He walks into the pub and looks around the busy bar and spots Wendy in the corner. He walks over and says, "Sorry I'm late, darlin'. I had a bit of a hold-up to contend with. What can I get you?"

"A large Pinot, and make sure it's nice and cold. I got so hot walking around the market." Jack walks to the bar.

The barman, who is skinny-looking with a pencil moustache, says, "What can I get for you, sir?"

"One large Pinot, and make sure it's cold, or I will get told off by the missus, and a large scotch and dry ginger, please, barman, no ice."

The barman says, "Certainly, sir." He pours the drinks and says, "That will be £13.75, please, sir. Is that it, or was there anything else?"

Jack, standing with a twenty-pound note in his hand, says, "How much?" not believing how much the drinks cost. Just then, there was a news flash on all the television screens around the bar.

The news reporter says:

"Breaking News! A daring bank robbery has taken place in Islington this morning by a two-man team. The police suspect it is part of a larger London gang. It appears that no one was physically injured. A spokesman for Scotland Yard said they used a clever plan to gain entry, obviously the work of professionals. The haul is estimated to be more than 8 million pounds in used banknotes. That's all we have for now; we will give you more on this story on the early evening news."

The barman turns to Jack and says, "You can't believe how clever these London boys are. Over 8 million, that's a hell of a lot! You have got to admire their nerve, haven't you? They walked in and took over 8 million, and nobody got hurt; that's what you call a professional job. Londoners, you can't beat 'em."

Jack swings around and hands the barman the twenty-pound note and say, "Yes, you're right; they are extremely daring, these London criminals. There's nobody where I come from who would even dream of taking that sort of risk. Have one yourself, barman."

"Thank you very much, sir. I will have a half with you. Here's your change; enjoy your drink. The Pinot is nice and chilled, so you won't get told off."

Jack says, "Cheers, mate." He picks up the drinks and walks over to Wendy, smiling to himself. He can't believe what he has just heard. All that practice on the cockney accent had worked a treat. He hands Mary her drink, sits down, and says, "Well, darlin', how did your morning go? Did you find your way around all right?"

"Yes, but everything in London is so expensive. I didn't buy a lot."

"Tell me about it. I have just had to have a bank loan to pay for these drinks." He smiles to himself. "Oh well, it's only money, and you are a long time dead. At least the museum was free."

"Well, after all these years of talking about going to the War Museum, did it live up to your expectations? I still can't imagine anybody getting excited about wartime stuff."

"It was very exciting, believe it or not. A lot of guns and all that stuff, so yes, I would say it did more than live up to my expectations. The courage of some of those guys was outstanding. I would like to think I would have that sort of courage in that sort of situation. Do you think I would have been a great soldier; would I have been a hero, you know blowing up railways, singlehandedly capturing prisoners, ordering people around? What do you think, Wendy?"

"Dream on, Jack, dream on. What time should we leave in the morning? I'm not all that keen on this place; it's too bloody hectic. Everybody is rushing around like headless chickens. I couldn't live at this pace. I really don't know how they do it; it's like a madhouse from what I can see of it. The sooner we go, the better, as far as I am concerned. What about you?"

"Yes, I agree; it's bloody crazy the way everybody is in a tearing hurry. Let's get back on the canal where we can relax. I thought we would get an early start around about six o'clock."

Wendy says, "That's bloody early! You were in a hurry to get here, now you are in a hurry to get out of here. What's the rush all of a sudden?"

"No, sweetheart, I am not in a rush, but one of the old boatmen tipped me the wink that the locks get very busy in the mornings, and if you don't get away early, you can be held up for hours. One hold-up is enough."

"Okay, I suppose you're right; you usually are. As long as you let me lay in until eight o'clock. I must admit I sleep really well on the boat; it must be the swaying of the water as other boats go by." Jack thinks, *I wish I fucking well did.*

"No problem. I just want to get out of London to the open countryside where we can relax and enjoy the tranquillity of nature; this place is nuts. I think we can be clear of London by about lunchtime tomorrow."

Wendy says, "By the way, what did you mean, one hold-up is enough?"

"Don't you remember when that lock got damaged and we had to wait until it got fixed? How could you forget that? I thought that was going to ruin all my plans for seeing the museum, but luckily, it didn't."

"Oh, that hold-up. Well, I thought you enjoyed that hold-up. You didn't seem to mind at the time. I think you made that old lockkeeper a bit jealous; he didn't believe a word of that bullshit about you sorting out your tackle for one minute. I bet he was glad to see the back of us."

"No, darlin', not that part of the hold-up, but we don't want to have to stop anywhere that we don't have to, especially here. So, the early start will ensure we get out of the city without any unnecessary delay, that's all it is."

"Yes, you're right, Jack. You can keep London for me. I am a country girl at heart. I could never live anywhere bigger than Rugby. It suits me; it's a lovely little town. Five minutes in the car and you are in open countryside. I know where everything is and where to get it. Up here, I would be like a fish out of water."

"I know, darlin', but these people don't know any different; they just adapt to the way it is. That's how they handle it. If you had been born here, you would find small towns like ours boring and dull."

In the meantime, back at the bank, Detective Superintendent Kelly is questioning the manager and his staff about the robbery. He is not at all happy with the slackness of the security and the way the robbers gained access.

"Well, Mr Green, I understand you are the manager of this department, and you are responsible for the day-to-day running of this department of the bank, is that correct?"

"Yes, I am the manager. I have been the manager here for the past twenty years or so. I can't believe that this has happened. We are all very shaken up. I am still shaking at the thought that any one of us or more than one of us could have been brutally murdered."

"Did you get a good look at them? Can you describe them to me? You know, age, height, eye colour, what they were wearing, those sorts of things. Please give me as much detail as you can, anything helps; you would be surprised how little clues have solved some of the biggest crimes. That's why we need statements from everybody involved while it is still fresh in their minds."

"Yes, but I honestly don't think it will be of much help to you; they were very well disguised."

"Let me be the judge of that, sir; carry on and try to relax and focus your mind on exactly what happened. Anything can help…"

"Well, let me think, they wore black baseball caps and dark glasses. They both had full beards, and they both had dark blue overalls; I think you call them boiler suits. Black gloves and shoes. Both had Cockney accents; they were both about five foot eight tall, and they both had short, barrelled shotguns. It all happened so fast; I am sorry I can't be more helpful. I was so scared; I know they would have killed us if we hadn't done as we were told. They were definitely serious, well-experienced criminals, you could tell. Just their nasty, East End- sounding language was enough to scare me and my staff, even if they weren't carrying guns. I'm afraid we lead a very sheltered life in the banking community; it's not something that happens to people like us. You are involved in this sort of thing daily, but we don't expect to come to work and be faced with hardened criminals. So maybe now you can appreciate the state of shock we are all in."

"Yes, I am sure they would have killed to get their hands on the sort of money they came for; of that I have got no doubt. You did exactly the right thing by complying with their demands, not a time to start playing the hero. Now how do you think they gained entry? Because I can't believe it was possible for them to just walk in like it appears they did."

"I take your point, Officer. Now that this has happened, it does seem ridiculous that in this day and age our security is so very old-fashioned, to say the least.

"It seems that they knew the password, which changes twice a day, once in the morning and once in the afternoon. They said they were early with the delivery; they obviously knew by doing that they had twenty-five minutes before the real delivery arrived. Apparently, they put a sign by the intercom saying that we were having a fire drill and that it would delay the next real delivery by a further thirty minutes. You have got to say they really planned every eventuality, giving them the best possible chance of getting in and out without interruption. They gave the password, and they knew Julie's name. Julie believed them and let them in. One of them held a gun to her head and threatened to kill her if we didn't do as we were told.

"When they left, they said if we raised the alarm, we would be responsible for her death. They said they were taking her with them, and they would kill her if they heard on their police radio scanner that we had raised the alarm within one hour of them leaving the bank. They said they would ring and tell us where she was when they left her, which they did.

"We all felt so very stupid when we found out they had tied her up and put her in the dumpster. If only we had known, we would have raised the alarm the second they left the bank, but we didn't know. I suppose you have got to admire their nerve and their detailed planning and the fact that nobody got hurt."

"It sounds to me like a very well-organised professional outfit; more than likely local villains from the East End, or they could be from the other side of the river; it will be one or the other. Right, Mr Green, we will take statements from all of you. But it doesn't sound like that will give us a great deal to go on from what you have already told me. I think the lesson to be learnt here is that the bank needs to bring its security procedure into the 21st century. I have never seen anything so slack in all my years on the job. Especially with the amount of money you deal with here on a daily basis. It's unbelievably slack."

"I am afraid you're right, Detective. In all the years I have been manager here, nothing has ever been upgraded. I suppose the reason is because nothing like this has ever happened here before, so it has been neglectfully overlooked. I feel a lot more should have been done to upgrade the system. But as we all know, hindsight is perfect vision. If only we could have seen this coming; it could have so easily been avoided."

"I suppose you're right. It's always the same old story; nothing gets done until something happens. It's an expensive lesson, over 8 million, a very expensive lesson indeed. Our crime prevention division will be in touch with the bank to give advice. Well, that's about it for now. I will let you get on with sorting things out. I think it will be a while before you will be able to resume operations around here."

"Thank you, Officer. I am closing the department, and I will send all the staff home when you have taken their statements. They're all very shaken up and shocked, especially Julie. I will give her paid leave to give her some time to get over the trauma she has been through; she will probably need therapy of some sort. She must have been petrified by the way she was treated by those thugs. It was unbelievably cruel treating a young girl like that; it will probably scar her for life."

Meanwhile, Jack and Wendy are back on the boat. After a night of practically no sleep and paranoia running riot in Jack's head about police raids or thieves stealing the money at any minute, he sets off for home, chugging out of Camden at daybreak. He looks back at all the moored boats with smoke coming out of their chimneys, thinking, *Did we really do it? Two old builders on the verge of bankruptcy two days ago, and now we are millionaires, and the only two people on the planet who know that are me and Frank; nobody would believe it even if we told them. When it was announced on last night's national news, everybody in the country will think it's part of a London gang that did it. Well, I did tell Frank that with meticulous planning and a bit of luck, we could do it, and we did.*

Two hours later, he moors up, makes two cups of tea, wakes Wendy and hands her a cup, saying, "Look out of the window, sweetheart."

Wendy looks out and says, "Oh, Jack, green fields and open countryside; we don't realise how lucky we are to have this sort of freedom. They can keep London. I don't care if I never go there again. How about you, Jack?"

"Yes, you're right. I feel the same as you. I don't know how people can live there; it's too fast; it would drive me mental. Well, it doesn't get much slower than chugging down the Grand Union Canal, does it? My darling, drink your tea, and I will make us some breakfast."

Later that day back at the office, Frank is fending off creditors, all the while thinking how bizarre it all is. He thinks, *Here I am, trying to steer the business through turbulent waters, and somewhere on the Grand Union Canal, Jack is steering towards me with a fortune on board the aptly named Victory. What a fucking surreal situation to be in! I can hardly believe it; it all feels like a distant dream. I had better get down to the allotment and carry on digging the hole under the shed to create our mini vault, well, rusty old water tank ready for when Jack gets back with the booty.*

That evening, Frank is busy digging as he is piling up soil at the back of his shed when his next-door neighbour, nosey Ernie, shouts across to Frank, "What are you doing, Frank, mining for gold?"

Frank startles; he didn't think anybody was around. He shouts back, "Hello, Ernie, I didn't see you there. I am just building a bank to keep the rats out; they're a bloody nuisance; they seem to chew any bloody thing. They even chewed my Wellingtons, the little bastards."

"If you're building a bank, you had better build a good one, not like the one that has buggered your business up."

"Oh yes, I see what you mean, Ern. Those sorts of banks, they can't keep the rats out of them; they're full of dirty fucking rats. They need exterminating, the bastards. Well, that's enough for tonight. I've worked up a thirst. I am going to the Bull for a well-earned pint. Goodnight, Ernie," Frank says, thinking, *Nosey old bastard.*

"Goodnight, Frank; you might get lucky and find some gold; you never know. Keep your pecker up."

"The chance would be a fine thing, Ernie," Frank says and pretends to laugh.

Back on the Victory, forty miles out of London, Jack is steering the boat. Wendy brings him a sandwich and a glass of wine, saying, "Are you all right, Jack? You seem preoccupied. What are you thinking about? Is it all the trouble you are going back to with the business? Is that what's troubling you?"

"Something like that, sweetheart; it just all seems so bloody unfair the way the banks can treat long-established businesses like ours. They must be trained to not think of the human beings behind the bloody bank statements. All the people who rely on me and Frank for a weekly wage. It's them and their families, as much as everything else that upsets me the most."

"Come on, Jack Redman, this is not like you. It'll sort itself out eventually; it always does. Eat your sandwich and drink your wine; you will feel all the better for it." Wendy kisses Jack on the cheek.

"Yeah, you're right as usual, but I do feel bad for your sake as well; you don't deserve this. I feel like I have let you down, and you're the last one in the world I would want to let down! I suppose we have had it good for a long time; that's why I think it will hurt when the crunch finally comes."

"Don't be daft; we have been poor before. We were poor when we got married, and we were happy then. We will manage somehow. The one thing I have learnt from you, Jack, is how to duck and dive. I have seen you doing it ever since I met you, and some of that has rubbed off on me. That's why I know we will be all right whatever they throw at us; they can't put the Redmans down. We will never surrender, will we?"

"No, I guess you are right; we will never give in without a bloody good fight; that is the Redman way. I do love you, Wendy. I want you to know you have been a fantastic wife and a wonderful mother to our two kids. Whatever happens, I want you to know that. I will always love you, no matter what."

"Now then, Jack, you're talking as if we won't be together. I don't like it when you get serious. It's not like you. Come on, where's Jack the Joker? Snap out of it. Let me get you another glass of wine. I can't have you getting melancholy; that would never do."

"Yes, my dear Wendy, you are quite right. I don't suppose we will starve. And besides, we can always get something out of Frank's allotment if things get desperate." He laughs.

"I don't think we would get anything worth having off of that old veg patch. I think Frank only keeps it on so he can go and relax and read the paper in his shed. And then he goes to the Bull for a drink with you, and his poor wife thinks he is breaking his back digging. He probably buys some veg on the way home. Frank can be very crafty when he wants to."

"You might be surprised what Frank can produce out of his allotment. It might be enough to keep us going for a bit. Anyway, let's stop at that nice pub we stopped at on the way down for dinner. What was it called? The Opposite Lock, wasn't it?"

"That sounds more like the man I know and love…never forgets a pub. Yes, why not? Life's too short to worry. But it's not The Opposite Lock; that's the nightclub we used to go to near the canal in Birmingham. It's The Old Lock Gate."

"Of course it is. That was a flashback; we had some rare old times over there back in the day. I wonder if it's still open? We should find out and give it a go for old times' sake."

"Don't get kidding yourself, Jack; our nightclubbing days are over. We would look well out of place in a nightclub; besides, it probably closed down years ago."

Later that day, they moor up near the pub and walk down the towpath. It's a lovely, sunny evening; the birds are singing, and a pair of swans glide by. Jack says, "I don't know what got into me earlier. How wonderful is this? We should count our blessings. You don't need diamonds and pearls when you have got all this for free."

"That's more like it, Jack. Come on, let's make the most of this holiday; it will be over before much longer. And then we will have to take a deep breath and face the music. But not yet, so let's seize the moment and enjoy ourselves now."

They enter the pub and manage to find a nice table for two, overlooking the canal. They browse the menu and decide to go for a steak with all the trimmings, topped off with a pepper sauce and a bottle of chardonnay. It's now eight o'clock, and Wendy and Jack are enjoying their dessert of Eton Mess.

Wendy says, "This is a lovely pub. I wish it was a bit nearer to our place; if it was, we would come here often. It's just got something about it. The food is good, it's not too pricey and the atmosphere is just right."

"Yes, that would be nice; it's nice to see somewhere doing well in these hard times. Mind you, I bet it's dead in the winter, when all the holiday boats are moored up. I suppose you will get some trade from elsewhere, but it does rely heavily on canal boats. Maybe they close in the middle of winter and bugger off abroad."

"Yes, it would be; it's all canal trade. There's nothing else around here. But as you say, it's a little gold mine for at least eight months of the year. So, you could be right; they might have a house in Spain or somewhere where they hibernate in the winter months. It wouldn't be a bad way of living: grab the cash and get some sunshine, yes, that quite appeals to me."

"Would you like to live abroad, Wendy, if we had a place? We nearly built one in Northern Cyprus once. Do you remember when me and Frank went over there to look for land? It turned out that it was a bit risky at the time. The Turks and the Greeks were still throwing things at each other, so we decided against it. But would you like to live in a sunny country if we could?"

"Well, Jack, the way things are now, there is not much chance of that. But yes, I think I could enjoy living abroad if we had the money to have a nice place, preferably with a pool. Stop dreaming, Jack; that's not going to happen, is it?"

"You never know, we might win the lottery. There is always hope, Wendy. There is always hope."

They can't help overhearing a couple of guys talking on the next table with a country accent.

The First Guy: "Did you hear about that bloody bank robbery in London a few days ago? Those London gangsters are bloody good when it comes to organised crime. They've got some nerve when it comes to that sort of thing."

Second Guy: "Oh, you're right there. The buggers went in broad daylight, only two of them. They had shotguns, but it still would take nerves of steel to take that sort of risk. According to the news, they walked out with over 8 million quid, a record for armed bank robbery in this country, they said on today's news. Not a bad day's work; perhaps we had better dust off our old guns and give it a go." They both laugh.

First Guy: "Well, I say good luck to them; it's about time somebody gave the banks a dose of their own medicine. The biggest robbers are the banks and the bankers with their big fat cat bonuses. That's daylight robbery without violence. They have buggered the country up, and they still have the nerve to take huge bonuses. That's bloody criminal in my book, and us taxpayers have to foot the bill. I hope they get away with it; as you said, nobody got hurt. They obviously knew what they were doing; it couldn't have been the first bank they had robbed."

"Did you hear that, Jack? They are talking about those bank robbers as if they were some kind of modern-day Robin Hood types. Whatever next? I can't believe they are praising thugs with guns who could have killed innocent people going about their honest hard-working jobs."

"Well, they have got a point. Look how the bank has treated us. It's about time they got a bit of their own back. Good luck to them, I say. I think Robin Hood would have been proud of them if they were around back in those times. I hope they get away with it. Come on love, eat your dinner."

After a 30-second pause, Wendy says,

"Well, I suppose you have got a point; the banks do need a bit of a lesson, and nobody got hurt…and they do sound like a cheeky pair of rogues. Yes, I hope they get away with it as well."

"Well, I will drink to that, sweetheart." Jack finishes his drink and thinks, *If only you knew who the two cheeky rogues were and that you were chugging down the Grand Union with one of them; and with over 8 million in stolen booty in the front locker.*

"Jack, you would drink to anything. I suppose you want another?"

"Well, I'm sure you could twist my arm; we are on holiday, after all. Why don't we have a bottle of Prosecco? We both like that, and this is our last dinner of the holiday, so let's push the boat out, pardon the pun."

"Oh, I suppose so, only if my credit card is still working though. I might as well max it out if we are about to go bust, and rob the bank as well as those London lads while I'm at it."

"Good idea, sweetheart. I never thought of maxing out the cards. I will do the same, and I will tell Frank and Mary to do the same, why not?"

The card works to pay for all the evening's food and drink.

They enjoy the Prosecco, then they leave The Old Lock Gate Pub and walk down the towpath to the Victory, where Jack insists on a nightcap or two. Jack finally gets a good night's sleep. Not so good for Wendy, what with Jack's loud drunken snoring.

The next day, it's a lovely sunny morning. Jack drags himself out of his bed to the smell of bacon cooking. "Well done, sweetheart. I can't believe I have slept in; that was the best night's sleep I have had in a long time. How about you?"

"Not really, there was some bloke making a hell of a noise all night; it went on and on! What a bloody row!"

"Well, I never heard anything. Did you find out who it was?"

"It was you, you daft bugger, snoring like a pig all night. I'm not surprised you slept well; you drank enough to knock an elephant over by the time you went to bed."

"Sorry, darlin', but I needed a good night's sleep. I haven't slept like that for months. And now I am ready for a country breakfast."

"You don't deserve it, but I suppose you did need a good night's rest; it will do you good. I know you're worried about what's going to happen next, but we will deal with it when it happens. If there's nothing we can do to save the firm, we might as well stop worrying about it."

"I suppose you're right; you usually are. Thank God I have you on my side, or I really would be in a state; that's a fact."

They finish breakfast. Jack takes a shower while Wendy washes up. Jack comes out of the shower naked and grabs Wendy from behind, and yes, you have guessed it: the boat was a rocking. An hour or so later, Jack starts the engine and heads towards home. Only one more day to go after today, and then Jack has the problem of getting the money off the boat without Wendy knowing; that is something to think about! All that day, his mind was on getting the money off the boat and under Frank's shed.

And there was the little matter niggling in the background of the firm being on the brink of meltdown. That was another bridge to cross that wasn't going to be pleasant by any stretch of the imagination. That evening, they moored up and had a cosy meal and a couple of bottles of cheap but pleasant white wine on the boat. They watched a bit of telly and retired early, as Jack wanted to get an early start the next morning.

It's another lovely, sunny morning, and Jack makes his early start, determined to get the pride of the fleet back to Brinklow Wharf on time. By early afternoon, they are within a couple of miles of Rugby Golf Club, that skirts the canal bank near their house. Wendy brings Jack a sandwich and says, "Well, everything is clean and tidy, as we found it. I have packed the cases so we shouldn't have any trouble handing her back to our friend Billy."

"Well done love. I have been thinking it would be a good idea that when we get to the golf course, I drop you off and you can walk up to the house and organise dinner in time for me getting back. I will take the boat back to Brinklow; it's not very far, and it's silly for us both to go when we are passing the house. I think I will be okay. In this last little section, there are no locks, so it will be easy on my own. I will get back by seven o'clock, so you can have the dinner ready for then; that would be great. It would be nice to come home to a nice, cooked dinner after being cooped up in this small boat for two weeks."

"Well, if you are sure you will be all right; it would make sense. I don't like leaving you on your own, but I suppose it's not far, is it? Seven o'clock, you said; that's quite late; you should be back before then, surely."

"Well, it might be earlier; that depends on how long it takes Billy to inspect the pride of the fleet for any damage. I think he will be very thorough, as it is his pride and joy. That could take some time at the speed he moves at. And then I have got to get the luggage into the car and drive back to Rugby."

"You don't have to make it sound like you are birthing the Queen Mary 2. I know you, Jack; you are popping in your second home for a pint. All right, I will see you when I see you as usual. If Frank's there, it will probably end up being supper. If you do see him, and I am sure you will, mention to him about them both maxing out their credit cards; that's if they haven't already done it."

Twenty minutes later, Jack moors up at the golf course, helps Wendy get off the boat, and kisses her goodbye. Jack casts off and waves to Wendy as she walks up the slope of the golf course towards home.

Wendy shouts, "You be careful; it's tricky on your own. I will see you later. Not too much later, Jack, you will have me worrying that you have sunk. Give me a ring when you are in the Bull, to put my mind at rest!"

"Okay, sweetheart, I will, but don't worry, I will be fine."

Jack heads for Brinklow and phones Frank.

"How are you doing, mate? I have just dropped Wendy off at the golf course. And I am on my way to the boatyard. How are things with the business?"

"Not good; we have got no chance. The way the bank is talking, there is no sign of them giving us any mercy, the bastards."

"Well, I am not surprised after meeting that slimy bastard in their head office in London. You could tell they were feeding us a load of bullshit. Anyway, fuck them; we don't need them anymore. We found a much more sympathetic bank, eh, Frank? Anyway, is everything ready to receive the cargo at the allotment? We won't need a bank when we have got money in the tank. Nice little rhyme, eh, Frank?"

"You can't help it, can you? Always Jack the Joker. Yes, it's all sorted. What time will you meet me there? I will feel much happier when the cargo is in the hold, and we are in the Bull having a debriefing session. My nerves are about shot, what with juggling the firm and worrying about you getting back in one piece."

"Same here, mate. I have been sleeping with one eye open for a week. I'm about knackered trying to pretend I am a carefree holidaymaker so that Wendy wouldn't suspect anything was up, some fucking holiday. I will ring you when I leave the boatyard, then it will take me about twenty minutes to get to the allotment. It's going to rain later, which should keep everybody away from the allotments, so nobody will see us stashing the cash."

"Okay, Jack, I can't wait to see you back safe; it seems like ages since we did our visit to the capital city to rearrange our financial affairs with a more giving bank."

"Okay, mate. I am looking forward to us having a couple of pints in the Bull later. See you soon. Cheers!"

Jack arrives at the boatyard, very relieved to be back with the mission complete. It could so easily have been a one-way trip. He spots Billy and shouts, "Hi, Billy, I am back with the pride of the fleet, and she has performed exactly as you said; it has been a pleasure skippering her. She is exactly the same as she was when I left two weeks ago; you taught me well."

"I will be the judge of that, my boy. They all say that you would be amazed at what damage the bastards do and won't admit it. I have more arguments over that than you can imagine. Some of the stories they come up with would make your hair curl. Anyway, let's have a good look over her and see if you have to start thinking of a story to tell me."

Twenty minutes later, Billy says, "Well, I have had a good look around her, and I am pleased to say she looks fine. I see you have got a lot more baggage than when you left. Where is the wife, have you left her in London? Or has she run off with a handsome lockkeeper?"

"No, she is in the extra cases; we had a row, and I won! Only joking; I dropped her off on the way through Rugby at the golf course. We live right by there; she walked home from there. And the extra bags we got at Camden Market, and the missus soon filled them. She is a shopaholic; there was no stopping her, but we were on holiday, so why not?"

"Oh, I see. I would rather be an alcoholic than a shopaholic, eh, Roy?"

"Every time, Billy, so everything is in order, then? I can go without having to make up a story it seems!"

"Yes, everything seems to be in ship shape and Brinklow Fashion—just my little joke. I made that up myself; not bad, eh, Roy? I do come up with the odd one now and again."

"Very clever, Billy; that must have taken some doing to think that one up. Well, I will be on my way; it's been an absolute pleasure. It really has been a great holiday. Look after the old girl; I might be back next year to take her for another trip," says Jack while thinking to himself, *No fucking chance. A nice yacht in the med would be more my style; you can keep the shitty canals from now on.*

"Okay, shipmate, I am glad you enjoyed the trip; I enjoyed the grand in the hand," says Billy, laughing.

Jack loads the car up and sets off to meet Frank at the allotment. Travelling back down the Brinklow strait, he rings Frank.

"Hi, Frank, I am on my way back. I will see you in twenty minutes at the allotment."

"Okay, I will be there waiting for you. Cheers."

As Jack slips the phone into his pocket, he feels shock horror, as he spots blue lights in his mirror, and then the siren screams, and the police car overtakes him and pulls him into a layby. Jack is convinced he is about to be arrested for the bank job; he pushes the button and drops the window.

The police officer walks to the car. Jack is desperately trying to keep calm. The policeman says, "Good afternoon, sir, did you know it is an endorsable offence, which also carries a two hundred pound fine, for using a mobile phone while you are driving?"

"Yes, Officer, I must admit I did know that. I am very sorry. I can assure you it's not something I do as a rule. I've just come back from a long business trip, and I was ringing my wife to tell her a white lie. I told her that I had been delayed and that I couldn't get back for her 50th birthday party. I was planning to turn up with a big bunch of flowers and surprise her."

"Well, next time you want to make a phone call, pull over, switch off your engine and then you can legally make your call. Now I don't want to spoil your wife's birthday by sending you home miserable, so I am going to let you off with a warning this time. Don't let me catch you again. Now go and surprise your wife."

"Thanks a million, Officer. I really am grateful, and I won't do it again, I promise."

"Make sure you don't." The policeman goes back to his car and drives off. Jack sits for a minute, trying to stop shaking; he can't believe he hasn't been arrested. He drives off and pulls into the Queen's Head and downs a double whisky. He sits still in silence for about five minutes, takes a deep breath and goes to the car, takes another deep breath, turns the key and drives off. Fifteen minutes later, he arrives at Frank's allotment. Frank walks to the car and says, "Are you all right, mate? You look like you have seen a ghost. I've never seen you so pale and shaky."

"I should think I am pale and fucking shaky."

"Why, what happened?"

"I was driving down the Brinklow strait about thirty minutes ago. I was on the phone with you, and I had just finished when I clocked blue lights in my mirror, then I heard the dreaded siren. Everything flashed through my mind. I thought the game was up; the last thing on my mind was using the phone. Well, they pulled me into the layby and gave me a good bollocking. I returned fire with a cartload of bullshit, and amazingly, they let me off. I couldn't believe it. I couldn't believe I held my nerve; that's one thing the bank job has taught us- to keep calm in a crisis. I couldn't start the car, I was so shaky. When I eventually did, I drove straight to the Queen's Head at Bretford and had a double whisky."

"Any excuse for a drink! Only joking, mate; you got away with it, that's the main thing. Now you're safely back, so try and calm down. Just think how it's been for me this last week, trying to keep all the balls in the air running the business and at the same time worrying about whether you are going to get back with the loot or not."

"Sorry, mate, I have been too preoccupied with trying to drive the boat and act normal in front of Wendy. What did you do with the guns?"

"I took them to pieces and chucked the bits in different parts of the quarry, along with the Motorola flip phone."

"Well done, Frank; that's the way—no clues, no convictions. We must stick to that rule for the rest of our lives. Right, is there anybody around?"

"No, the rain has kept everybody away, so we are clear to put the cash in our Mickey Mouse vault unnoticed by the nosey bastards that are usually down there."

Frank and Jack put the money in the tank under Frank's allotment shed floor, lock the tank, fix the floorboards down, and cover them with the old mat. They lock the shed and go to the Bull for a couple of pints, and a quiet chat about everything that's going on with the business and its imminent demise. Eventually, the two leave the Bull, and Jack arrives home at last. He unloads the luggage and receives a mild bollocking from Wendy for being late, which he accepts gracefully; nothing new there.

It's Sunday lunch. Jack is enjoying a few pints with his mates in the Bull, with lots of the usual banter going on. Jim asks Jack, "How was the world cruise, then, Jack?"

"Don't take the piss. If you must know, it was a great trip. I wouldn't have missed it for anything. I never dreamt a canal trip could be so rewarding. You should try it sometime, Jim. Don't knock it until you have tried it."

Jerry chirps in, "Bullshit, Jack, how could a trip on a narrowboat be great? After all the world travel you have done over the years, there can be no comparison, surely?"

"Well, it had its moments, I can tell you."

Boozy Brian has to butt in, "What was that, Jack? Did you get arrested for speeding or loitering?"

"Stop taking the piss; it really was a cracking holiday, lots of open countryside and then the hustle and bustle of London. It certainly wasn't dull, and we managed to bring back some nice souvenirs from London to remember it for the rest of our lives. Anyway, lads, it's been nice listening to you all taking the piss. If I don't go now, my dinner will be in the dog, so I will see you later."

Harry, the landlord, shouts to Jack, "Take no notice there, only pulling your leg, mate; you know what they're like."

Jack leaves the pub, and his mates continue to talk about him.

Jerry remarks, "He puts a brave face on it, but it must be tough. All the money he has had for years and now he is going through shit; we shouldn't be too hard on him."

Boozy Brian says, "Don't worry about Jack; he is made of rubber. He will soon bounce back; he always does."

Jim says, "A bit like his cheques, eh, lads?"

Jerry goes on the defensive.

"Don't knock him; he is a good mate; he has helped us all out at one time or another. So don't knock the man when he is down."

Jim apologises, "Sorry, Jerry, you are right; I am out of order. He has been a good mate to every one of us when we have needed it. But you're right about him being made of rubber; he will bounce back. I wouldn't be surprised if he hasn't already got some fiendish plan going on in the background. Jack has always got something up his sleeve."

It's Monday morning. Frank arrives at the office; there are three strangers waiting by the door. Frank approaches the three men and says, "Who are you guys, and what are you doing here?"

The older man walks forward. "We are bailiffs, and we are here to serve an order of the court to take possession of this building and all the contents within. And may I ask who you are?"

"I am the joint managing director of Parker-Lake-Homes Limited. My name is Frank Harrison. And I know you can't enter the building by force; you can only enter the building if we allow you to. And we are not letting you in so you might as well fuck off right now."

"I am afraid you have got that wrong, Mr Harrison; we have got a legal possession order granted to my company by the high court. I know what you are talking about, but this is a possession that is enforceable. I don't like doing possessions, but I am afraid it has to be done. So I suggest you hand me the keys, or we will break in. We are going to change the locks anyway."

Just then, Jack drives up. He jumps out of his car and shouts, "What the fuck is going on here, Frank? Are these guys who I think they are? The fucking bailiffs?"

"Yes, they are Jack, and the bastards have got a court order to enter the place and change the locks so we can't get in. Basically, they are closing the business down. It seems like they have got the authority to do it from the High Court, or so they say."

"They can't do it, Frank. I will call the police. They can't just turn up unannounced and take our property; it can't be right. I am calling the police; they will sort this out for us."

The bailiff says, "Go ahead, they will tell you we are perfectly within our rights to carry out the lawful possession order. And change the locks, as I said earlier. I don't like doing repossessions; it's the worst part of our job, but we have to carry out the High Court's instructions. That's the way it works, and there is nothing you or the police can do about it."

Jack shouts, "I don't fucking well believe you, you bastards! You would say anything to get in." Jack rings the police.

After fifteen tense minutes, the police car pulls into the yard. The police officer gets out of the car and walks towards the gathering of squabbling men. "Now then, what seems to be the problem here?"

Jack says, "My name is Jack Redman, and this is Frank Harrison; we are joint managing directors of Parker-Lake-Homes Ltd. And these three bailiffs are telling us that they have the authority to take over our office building, change the locks and sell off all the contents. That can't be right, surely. They can't enter unless we let them in; that's the law, isn't it?"

"Well, it depends, sir; there are various types of orders the court can grant. There are different court orders for different reasons and particular situations; it is not as straightforward as you may think. Don't worry, I will get to the bottom of this, and if I can stop it, I will."

The older bailiff approaches the officer, shows him the possession order, and explains the situation.

The officer walks over to Jack and Frank.

"Well, I am sorry to have to tell you they are within their rights to carry out a legal possession. There's nothing I can do to help. I am afraid I can't stop them. I don't like this sort of thing, but my advice is to let them get on with it, or it will only get nasty and make things worse. I really wish I could help, but my hands are tied on this occasion. I'm sorry, chaps, I really am."

Frank says, "Okay, Officer, well, thanks for coming so quickly anyway. We know when we are beat, and we will take your advice and go quietly. Thanks for that. You have done your best, but the law is the law, and the last thing we would want to do is break the law; we are not that sort of people."

"No, sir, I am sure you're not. Anyway, I have got to go. Good luck to you both. I hope things turn out okay."

The officer drives away. Jack turns around, throws his office keys to the senior bailiff, and says, "Go on then, do your dirty work! It seems that you are within your rights, and to be fair, it's not your fault; it's the fucking bank that have caused this, the bastards."

The bailiff says, "We don't like this sort of thing, lads; it's happening far too often, especially in the house building sector. You are welcome to come in and collect your personal bits and bobs from your desks, etcetera. You're quite right; we are not the bad guys; it is as you so precisely put it: the fucking banks."

Frank and Jack go into their respective offices, empty their desks into carrier bags, and meet up in the boardroom. They both stand for a minute, staring at the illuminated presentation display showing some of the fine houses they had built over the last twenty-five years. Both start to well up.

Jack puts his head in his hands and wipes away the tears. Struggling to speak, he says, "Well, Frank, we never thought it would end like this. After all those years of hard work, this is what it has come down to. The bank letting us down in our time of need, and then without so much as a phone call, or at the very least an email to give us time to organise things, they send in the Gestapo, the bastards. If only I could get my hands on that two-faced little bastard we met in the head office of the bank in London, I would rip his fucking head off."

Frank picks up one of their many prestigious awards, looks at it, and says, "I know; I feel the same, mate. All for nothing. Come on, let's go. This is bloody heartbreaking. I can't take it in; it doesn't seem possible that they can just come and take our property from us without some sort of notice. But it seems they can. You heard what the copper said; they have the right to do it. It's at times like this that it seems to be a fine line between criminality and lawfulness. I am glad now that we took criminality; it serves the bastards right after this. I don't feel that we have done anything wrong."

"I agree, Frank; there doesn't seem to be much difference when you compare it to this situation. I am glad we did the other job. I don't feel any guilt after this fucking performance, none at all."

They walk down the drive carrying their bags, not quite believing what has happened.

"Don't look back, Frank; don't give them bastards the satisfaction of thinking that we are upset. We had better ring Karen and Mike and tell them what's happened and that we will be in touch when we know more about what's happening next. They will be upset, even though they knew it was coming. We knew it would happen; it was inevitable. Without the fucking bank behind us, we didn't stand a chance of surviving, but nevertheless, it still comes as a shock when it finally happens. It's like a knife in the back. Thank God, we did the other job and lived for another day."

Frank says, "I will meet you in the Bull at one o'clock if that's all right with you. We need to organise things and let people know what's going on. I think everybody who knows us will be surprised, especially all our subcontractors that we have given work to for all these years."

"Well, I think I could manage to meet you in the Bull, seeing as I have got fuck all else to do. Sorry, Frank, I didn't mean to shout. I just feel so fucking angry. Yes, of course I will see you at one. Cheers, mate."

It's ten minutes past one in the Bull. Jack has just been served. He walks over to where Frank is sitting and passes him his pint. "Here, find a good home for this and try not to cry in it." Jack sits down.

"Well, Frank, we knew it was going to happen, but that doesn't make it any easier to stomach. We have nursed the company along for all these years. I can't believe it's not there anymore; it doesn't seem possible somehow. It's like losing a limb. Or a close member of the family."

"I know what you mean, Jack. We knew it had to end, but when it does, it hurts just the same. I am gutted as well, and the way the bailiffs stormed in and just took over, it was unbelievable. I really am gutted; that's the only word to describe it."

"So am I, Frank, but let's look on the bright side. We have got a plan B up our sleeve; we mustn't lose sight of that. We have just got to think of it as our new role in life. And the first thing we have got to start looking at is getting the money moved and into a bank abroad. Anyway, we have got plenty of time for that later. We have got to meet Mike and poor Karen. I will ring them and tell them that we will meet them in here at 11:00 on Friday morning, and we will put them in the picture and square them up; that's the least we can do. In the meantime, think about where we go from here. I will see you in here on Friday. And for now, you can spend a lot more time at the allotment on guard duty, if nothing else."

"What's the hourly rate?" They both laugh.

"Oh, and get some money out of the vault for those two on Friday; we will give them two weeks' wages and their holiday pay, and another two hundred each as a going-away present."

They have a good old chinwag over a couple more pints, which makes them both feel a lot better.

Then, it's off to break the news to their other halves. Both the women knew it was imminent, and both took it on the chin like proper wives do. They were mentally prepared for rented properties and cheap cars; they had done it in the early days, so they just had to bite the bullet and put up with what lay ahead. There was no alternative as far as they were concerned. But of course, we knew different.

It's eleven o'clock on Friday in the Bull. Frank and Jack walk in and spot Karen and Mike sitting and having a drink. They walk over, and Frank says, "Well, I won't say this is nice because it's not good news by any means, but it is what it is. We knew it would come to this; it was just a matter of time after all. We have just got to deal with it; that's all there is to it. Here are your wages and your holiday pay, and a bit extra to keep you going for now."

"We would like to thank you both for sticking with us until the bitter end; there aren't many that would have put up with the shit you two went through. You could have walked away at any time, and a lot would have done. So we want you to know we appreciate the loyalty you have given to us both, and it goes without saying, we will give you both excellent references if and when you need them."

Jack says, "The administrators are Cox and Cox. I can't believe we are being wound up by a pair of Cox. They will be in touch with you shortly. Apparently, we can all get redundancy payments through the government redundancy scheme. They will send you the appropriate forms in due course, and if you need any info from us, just shout. Oh, and the bailiffs said you can go and empty your desks and collect any other personal stuff you have there. The administrator will be there all next week."

Frank says, "Right, now let us buy you a farewell drink; we can still manage that."

Frank fetches a round of drinks and sits down. He picks his pint up and says, "Here's to you, and I hope you get fixed up with another job quickly. You have both been great employees, so whoever takes you on will be very lucky to get you. It's just a shame the bank let us down in our hour of need, or we wouldn't be in this situation."

Karen replies, "I hope we do, but it won't be the same. You two have been great to work for; we will really miss the old firm. Well, here's to you two. At least we are young enough to start again, but you two are no spring chickens, are you? I just can't imagine you working for somebody else after being your own bosses for all these years."

Mike chirps up, "Now then, Karen, don't depress them more than they already are. They're not that old; mid-fifties is considered middle-aged nowadays."

"Sorry, chaps. Me and my big mouth. I am sure something will turn up. Well, I have got to go. Thanks for the drink and thanks for the money; we didn't expect that." Karen gets up and kisses Jack, Frank, and Mike on the cheek.

"Look after yourselves, lads. I wish you all the best of luck. I really do, and I hope things work out for all of you. See you around, and I will be in touch if I need that reference you mentioned."

Mike stands up a couple of minutes later.

"Well, I had better go; I have got to go and sign on. What a bloody game." He gets up and shakes hands with Frank and Jack.

"Cheers, Frank. Cheers, Jack, especially for the money. We didn't think you could afford to pay us. We are grateful for it, you know that. So, I suppose this is it then; it will seem funny not having you two guys around. It's been great working with you. I am going to miss you both; you have been good to me over the years. I will always be thankful for the way you have treated me. They broke the mould when they made you two; that's a fact. See you around, I hope."

Mike walks outside, pulls out his hanky and wipes his eyes.

Frank says, "That was bloody hard. I had a job to hold back the tears. I will miss those two; they have been like family."

"And me, Frank, but what can we do? Everything has gone tits up; let's face it. The old firm is finished, and there's nothing we can do about it now. So, we have just got to carry on regardless of the circumstances."

"I know, Jack, but it makes you feel so bloody useless, particularly where those two are concerned. Well, at least they got paid thanks to the long-term interest-free London loan, and they will get redundancy money from the government, as the law states. So will we, of course; it seems like the world has gone bloody mad..."

"You're right there, Frank. Do you fancy another drink?" Jack goes to the bar and orders two pints of best bitter.

The barmaid, Ann, says, "I've never seen you two in here at lunchtime before you're evening trade as a rule. I always look forward to having a chat with you two when it's early and quiet."

"Don't worry, Ann, you will be seeing a lot more of us now; me and Frank have retired."

Jack picks up the glasses and starts to turn around.

Ann says, "You have retired? Since when? You're pulling my leg, aren't you?"

"It's a long story, Ann. I will tell you another time."

Jack sits down.

"Cheers, Jack. Let's forget P.L.H. Ltd deceased and concentrate on getting the new firm moving on. Have you had any thoughts on how we can get the money sorted abroad? Our six months of laying low will flash by in no time, so we need to get on with organising things; it won't be easy moving all that money about. The bank job is just the start of the journey; we have got a long way to go to complete the job. Have you had any ideas, Jack?"

"Well, I have been giving it a lot of thought, but so far I haven't come up with anything substantial. How about you?"

"The only idea I've come up with was to talk to Ali, the Moroccan accountant we know, and ask him if we could bank it there. And to get it there, we could take a trip to Spain in the old mobile home, stuff the money in the mattresses, and go over to Tangier on the ferry then drive down to Marrakech to meet him. What do you think, Jack?"

"It sounds too risky to me, involving a practical stranger, and an Arab at that. No, I don't think that's one of your better ideas."

"I see your point, Jack. What about Captain Richards? He has got a small plane; he could fly us out of the country."

Jack laughs. "You must be joking, Frank. He is always pissed; he would probably crash, or we would end up in the wrong country. Not a good idea; there has got to be a way of rinsing the money. We will think of something, we always do. Do you want one for the road?"

"Why not? We have got nothing better to do. I think I could get used to this retirement lark. At least now that the worst has happened, the pressure is off. I feel like a heavy weight has been taken off of me. It was bloody stressful this last three months; it can't be good for you, the kind of stress we have been put through."

Frank goes to the bar. "Two pints of the usual, Ann, and take one for yourself, sweetheart."

"Thanks, Frank, and here's to a happy retirement."

"Retirement? Oh, yes, retirement. Cheers, Ann." Frank returns to the table.

"Frank, I have been thinking while you were at the bar, the old motorhome part of your plan sounds good to me. You were right; we could put the money in the mattress and drive down to Dover and go over on the ferry to France."

"And then what?"

"I don't know, but once we are in France, we could go anywhere in Europe or beyond. We need to do some serious research, but the motorhome could be part of the plan; it's the best idea so far. At least it's a start; that's if the old motorhome will." They both laugh.

They finish their drinks and get up to leave.

Harry, the landlord, shouts, "Don't work too hard, lads."

Jack shouts back, "Not much fear of that, Harry."

It's Monday morning, and Frank phones Jack at home. Frank's wife is in the room. "How are things?"

"Could be better; how about you?"

"I was down at the allotment yesterday, and there is a lot of bindweed; it looks like a big job, like the other job. I wonder if you could come and help me for a few hours shifting it?"

"Yes, it should be all right. Hang on, I will just check with Wendy…Sweetheart, Frank wants me to help him get rid of some bindweed at his allotment this morning, is that okay with you?"

"Yes, that's okay. Will you be back for lunch?"

"Probably. I will ring you and let you know. Yes, Frank, that's fine. What time will you be there? Okay, I will see you in an hour. I will need some gloves."

"I have got some in the shed you can have; see you in an hour down there."

Jack arrives at the allotment an hour later, parks the car and walks towards Frank's shed, passing Ernie's plot.

"Good morning, Ernie. How are your taters doing? Are they nearly ready?"

Ernie shouts, "Morning, Jack! Not yet, mate, but they're getting bigger every day; they will be really big in another two weeks."

"Well, you had better order some bigger trousers then."

"What's that, Jack?"

"Nothing, Ernie." Jack mumbles to himself, "Silly old fucker." He goes into the shed where Frank is sitting reading the paper and drinking a cup of tea.

"Morning, Jack."

"Morning, Frank. That silly old bugger next door, he will take root down here one of these days. Anyway, what have you summoned me to the boardroom for?"

"Get a cup of tea and sit down. I have got some good news. I have found a bank that will take our money with no questions asked. Although it is a bit of a long shot, I am not altogether convinced."

"Why, where is this bloody bank? In South Africa or some other far-flung part of the globe?"

"It's Croatia, Jack."

"Oh, yeah, and where the fuck is Croatia? I have never heard of it."

"It's part of the old Yugoslavia, which was part of the old Soviet bloc. Don't you remember they had a war with Bosnia? Anyway, the banks there will take large cash deposits from anywhere and open accounts. They need money to rebuild their economy after the war put the country on its knees."

Jack scratches his head. "What makes you so sure about this? It sounds like bullshit to me. And if they have another war with their unfriendly neighbours and lose, where will our money end up, then?"

"I must say I never thought of that, Jack. I suppose it does sound too good to be true, and we know from experience if it sounds too good to be true, it usually is. So, what the fuck are we going to do? This is a problem we never dreamt we would have. I did have another idea, but I don't think you would like it."

"Well, tell me anyway; we have got to bounce ideas off each other until we come up with a sound plan of action."

"Well, Jack, this is somebody we know we can trust, but it's up to you whether you agree or not. Your son Jay works in Geneva in Switzerland. He sells pensions, which must involve him dealing with banks; he might know someone who could help us. It's worth a phone call at least. What do you think, Jack? It can't do any harm just to ask him."

"No, Frank, I don't like involving him in case he got in trouble. His mother would never forgive me. That would cause me so much grief with Wendy, and obviously I wouldn't want to put my son and his family at risk either."

"Jack, I am not suggesting he gets involved. Just the name and number of somebody, that's all I am talking about, no more than that."

"Well, if you put it like that, I suppose it couldn't do any harm just asking for an introduction; he couldn't get in any bother just doing that, could he? Okay, we will give it a try, but if it's complicated and involves more from him than just an introduction, it's a no go, all right? I will give him a call."

Jack phones his son.

"Hi, Jay, how are things?"

"Good, thanks, Dad. How about you?"

"Well, son, let me put it like this: when it's sunny, it's great, but at the moment, it is pissing down."

"Oh, sorry to hear that. Mum told me about the business going bust. Is there anything I can do to help?"

"Well, there is one thing you might be able to help with. We are looking to come to Geneva to bank some funds that me and your Uncle Frank have managed to save without anybody knowing about. Not even your mother or Frank's wife knows anything about this money. It's cash now. We wondered if you know anybody in the banking world over there that wouldn't ask too many questions about where the money has come from and would open two accounts, one for me and one for your Uncle Frank."

"Well, as a matter of fact, there is a senior bank manager who is in my Masonic lodge. He is a good friend, and I know he would do it if I asked him; he owes me a favour. I got him a big client recently, but he would want between 3 and 5% for taking the risk. How much would you want to bank?"

"Ummm… Ummm… about four million pounds altogether."

The phone goes quiet.

"How much? Are you trying to wind me up? Where would you get that sort of money after going bust? How much are you really talking about?"

"I am not winding you up, son. It could be a little over four million. I am being serious. Can you help, or is it too much for your mate to handle? It's a long story of how we managed to get it, but we have got it. I will tell you how when I see you next. But needless to say, we need to find a good laundryman to give it a wash for us. Do you think this guy is reliable with that amount of money involved? We must be able to trust him completely; it's an awful lot of money."

"Yes, I am sure he would be able to deal with it. Bloody hell! You two never cease to amaze me. Let me know when you are coming over, and I will meet you and give you his business card, and then it's up to you. I daren't get involved; that's as much as I can do, Dad. I'm sorry I can't be of more help."

"I know, Jay. We don't want you getting involved; just an introduction, that's all we want from you. Give my love to the family and promise me not a word to your missus or your mother; that could be fatal!"

"Sure, I promise. Just you and Uncle Frank be careful. I don't know what you're up to, but it sounds bloody dangerous to me. See you soon and take care, you pair of old rascals."

"And you, son, and thanks for the help; you won't regret it. I am looking forward to seeing you your missus and the kids."

"Well, Frank, I think that went well. Jay is a good judge of human nature, and if this guy is in his Masonic lodge, he won't let Jay down. It isn't done in those sorts of circles, or at least, I hope not. It sounds a bloody sight better than your Croation idea anyway."

"That's great news, Jack. I think we should buy our two houses for about a million each. I have heard that people are desperate to sell abroad, and they will risk taking cash because they have got no confidence in the banks, just like over here. The bloody monetary system in Europe is in a state of chaos. And then when we have got the houses sorted, we will have safes installed and put a million in each of them. We can change money weekly at the tourist currency exchange points. Just a few hundred at a time, not enough to be noticed by anybody in authority, that is."

"That sounds like a good idea, Frank. I must say it never entered my head to keep that amount of money in the house, but having said that, we have got over 8 million stashed under a garden shed; based on that principle, nobody would believe anybody would be daft enough to keep that sort of money in a home safe. And the other 4.5 million can open the Swiss accounts. That's it, Jack, the plan is all set. All we need is God's speed and a lot of luck, and we are in the clear."

"I bet God's speed is faster than our old campervan."

"Well, Frank, we will have to think about that, but let's concentrate on buying the houses for now. I know you fancy Spain and I fancy Italy, Viareggio or at least somewhere on the Italian Riviera, that's where I want to be."

"I thought you were set on going to Northern Cyprus; you were going to get your mate over there to sort you a place out near him?"

"Not really, Frank, it was just the first thing I thought of, but I have had second thoughts. I don't think Wendy would like it; she loves Tuscany. Well, we both do. It's more civilised and cultured, the food and wines are better, the weather is great, and I know a few expats over there that live around that area. You remember Toby the solicitor? He lives near there. He will help me sort a nice villa out; he owes me a favour or two, and as we know from our dodgy deals in the past, he doesn't ask awkward questions. He is just the sort of contact I need. I bet he knows all the right people out there who can help. Toby is no mug, as we know by some of the stunts he has pulled for us when we have been buying building land."

"Well, I am surprised. I thought your mind was made up on Northern Cyprus. But having heard what you are saying about Italy and having Toby over there, it does sound like a good idea."

"Well, Frank, for one thing, it would be impossible for us to drive to Spain and then go to Northern Cyprus and Switzerland in two weeks to do the deals. It will be a fair old punch to do Spain, Italy and Geneva in two weeks, but it can be done. I am pretty sure you can buy a nice villa in Spain for cash; the market is completely fucked over there, I have heard. You will get a lot for your money. It's the same in Italy, according to the news, so I am sure Toby will find me a bargain with a million in cash to spend. I should get a real nice place with a swimming pool and all the trimmings."

"I think we should both get cracking places for that sort of money, especially with cash. We have always said cash is king, and it always will be. They reckon prices in Spain have dropped by half, and as you say, Italy is the same, which gives us a great advantage having the readies to spend. There's not many people that can lay their hands on that sort of money nowadays."

"Yes, Frank, I can see it now: the Redmans Retreat and Harrisons Hideaway." They both laugh.

"Oh God, Jack, I hope we can get away with this. It all seems so unreal, us sitting in a garden shed in England, literally sitting on eight and a half million pounds, talking about buying luxury villas abroad. Anyway, let's get back to reality. Let's both look for properties on the internet and carefully broach the subject of cash. There must be people out there that are desperate to sell anyway they can."

"Sounds good to me, Frank; we'll worry about how we get the money out there later. As we said the old campervan sounds favourite. We could drive to Spain and buy your place, and then drive to Italy and conclude my deal, and then straight to Geneva to sort out the bank, and then we are homeward bound. Sounds easy when you say it. But it is a hell of a task. I just hope we can pull it off."

"Well, that all sounds like it could work to me, Jack. Once we have got the properties lined up, we will go and do the deals. The next trick is to think of something to tell the girls as to why we suddenly want to bugger off to France for two weeks; that's not going to be easy."

"Well, we have got plenty of time to figure that one out; it's going to take at least two months to find the properties and set up the purchasing details. So, we say nothing for now, and by that time the dust will have settled a bit more. We will come up with some sort of cunning excuse to give to them. We're pretty good at cunning plans. I am afraid we have had to be."

About four weeks have gone by. Jack and Frank are well into negotiations on their property deals. Both the wives are trying to make ends meet living on state benefits and living in rented flats. They bump into each other while shopping in the market. Wendy invites Mary to join her for a cup of coffee in Wetherspoons, which is just across the road from the market. They walk in and find a table and settle down with their drinks for a chat.

"Well, Mary, how are things? Are you managing to keep your spirits up considering the drastic change in our circumstances?"

"Well, to tell you the truth, Wendy, I am struggling to adjust. It's like starting all over again, which was all right when I was a young girl, but it's bloody hard now that I am older. What about you? How are you finding it?"

"Pretty much the same, Mary. The trouble is, for years I haven't had to think about the cost of things, and now I have to watch every penny. There never seems enough to go around, but I never was very good with money."

"How is Jack taking it?"

"He seems pretty upbeat, but that's Jack; it takes a lot to get him down, although he has his moments when he goes quiet on me. I'm glad he's got Frank to lick his wounds with. They spend hours at Frank's allotment and, of course, hours in the Bull."

"But that's our boys for you. I am sure they will surprise us one day; they usually do. Perhaps this is the lull before the storm. Anyway, Wendy, it has been nice seeing you. We will have to do it again soon, but I must get on. I have got to get something for Frank's dinner. Bye for now."

"Bye, Mary, see you soon. It's been nice having a chat; let's not leave it so long until the next time. You know what they say: trouble shared is trouble halved. We should get together once a week to compare notes; that would be good therapy for us both."

"Yes, that sounds good. Just give me a ring and let me know when. You're right, it would do us both good to have a natter once a week. I like that idea. Well, see you next week then. Bye for now."

Frank and Jack meet in the Bull; it's approximately three weeks to the highly risky money run. Frank opens the conversation.

"How's your deal going with the Italian villa, Jack? Mine is sorted. I can't believe how casual the lawyers are over in Spain. And I had very little trouble sorting out a cash deal with the estate agent. It must be because they are so desperate to make a sale that they have lowered their professional standards, that's if they ever had any. They seem to want to do a deal any way they can. And I suppose their clients are prepared to do the same from what I can see of it. This bloody credit crunch, as they call it, seems to have spooked everybody into taking risks they wouldn't have taken prior to the banks causing havoc."

"Mine is pretty much the same, Frank, to be honest. Listen to me: 'to be honest', that's hardly an appropriate phrase, is it? But being serious, Toby has turned out to be an absolute winner. He has sorted everything out for me. We will stop with him for a couple of nights; his missus is a bit of all right; she will look after us well. I can't get over how much buying power cash has got; it just shows you what a mess the world of finance is in. Now then, have you thought of some plausible excuse we can tell the wives as to why we want to bugger off to France for a couple of weeks? It isn't going to be easy. I keep thinking of things, and there is always something that wouldn't work with one thing or another. How about you, Frank, have you come up with a brainwave?"

"Yes, Jack, I just might have. What do you think of this for a plan? I was talking to Les Boles the other day. You know him; he has worked for us before; he is a plumber. Anyway, I met him in the Railway Club, and he was boring me as usual, telling me all about his carp fishing exploits, and he happened to mention to me how popular it is in France. And how lots of Brits go over there to fish the lakes for record-breaking carp. He told me he had been over there lots of times with his lads to take part in competitions. Well, it suddenly struck me that we have done a fair bit of fishing in our time. So, I was thinking if we tell the girls that we have been invited to take part in an amateur competition with large cash prizes. Let them think we might come back with some cash, and I think they will go for it. Then we can go and do our whirlwind tour of Europe. Then when we come back with five grand as our winnings and tell them we got lucky, that should please them.

After all, since the firm fell on its arse, they haven't had much fun. Then we will treat them to a nice meal and give them five hundred each to treat themselves; that should give us the welcome home card. What do you think? It's the only thing I can think of that might work."

"I reckon it's a bloody brilliant idea. You don't come up with them very often, Frank, but when you do, you seem to find a bit of the Einstein factor. Well done. I'll start sorting my fishing gear out when I get home, and I know Wendy will ask me what's going on, and that's the time I will tell her I have heard about this competition and that me and Frank have decided to give it a go. And if you do the same, we stand a fair chance of getting away with it. Bloody brilliant, well done, Frank."

Three weeks later, both villas are ready for legal completion; they have only viewed them on the internet, but they are both satisfied that they have bought well. They have had substantial safes installed included in the price. So, this was it; the next big risk was about to begin. Lots of planning details were gone over again and again in the men's makeshift boardroom; the garden shed. All the next week, they were getting prepared. The ferry was booked for the Dover crossing, and the campervan was serviced. It was finally time to leave.

Frank loads the fishing tackle and a small suitcase. He kisses Mary goodbye; he cannot help but wonder whether he would ever see her again. He drives to Jack's house; it is 6:00 am and still dark. Jack chucks his suitcase and fishing tackle in the back of the camper. Wendy kisses Jack, and he gives her a hug and says, "Look after yourself, sweetheart."

She says, "Go on, you silly old bugger, go and catch a big fish and bring me some money back with you. Then you can have more than a hug and a kiss, I promise."

"That's the plan, darlin'; let's hope it works and I get the reward that you have promised." He thinks to himself, *If only she knew what we are really up to. God knows what they will make of the things we have done if our plan works, and we have to tell them the truth.*

Wendy waves them off. They drive straight to the allotment and fill the empty mattresses they had prepared the night before with their ill-gotten gains, all 8.5 million in twenty-pound notes. And they are off to Dover to start another nerve-racking adventure.

They are chatting on route to Dover.

"I can't believe we are taking this chance, Frank. It's nearly as nerve racking as when we did the job six months ago; it's all come flooding back to me. I had almost shelved any thoughts of the day of the bank robbery, and now I keep getting flashbacks; how about you?"

"Yes, the same, Jack; it isn't doing my digestion much good at all. I keep thinking, if we get caught with this lot on board, it will all have been all for nothing. Just let's pray we can get away with it; this is one of the most important parts of the job. It's all very well stealing it, but getting it street legal is just as difficult. But fuck it, we haven't got much choice; it wasn't doing any good under my shed at the allotment. We have got to go through with it no matter what the risk."

After the long drive, they enter the Dover ferry port; it is raining heavily.

"Well, Frank, this is it, here we go. Come hell or high water, as the nautical saying goes."

As they drive down the ramp towards the ship, a customs man, wearing a yellow hi-vis cape, steps out. Jack brakes, applies the handbrake and winds down the window.

The customs man asks for passports. Jack hands him the passports.

"Business or pleasure, gentlemen?"

Jack says, "Pleasure, we hope. We are going on a carp fishing holiday in France. It will bring us great pleasure if we can get some big fish. If not, it will be very boring."

The customs man hands back the passports and says, "Okay, follow the signs onto the ship. Hope you catch plenty of fish. I know what it's like when I go fishing and get bugger all."

Jack shouts, "Thanks, mate," and closes the window. He turns to Frank and says, "Yes, as long as they don't catch us first, eh, Frank?"

"Fuck me, Jack, that was easy. Well, I knew it had got a lot more relaxed since we joined the EU. I never liked the idea until now."

After a smooth crossing and a couple of nerve steadiers in the ship's bar, they drive onto French soil, straight through French customs, and they leave the port without any hassle. After about a four-hour drive, they stop for some coffee and cake at a service area. When they walk back to the camper, they spot a police motorcycle parked by the side of it. As they walk to get in, a policeman approaches and asks in fluent English, "Is this your vehicle?"

Frank says, "Yes, what is the problem, Officer? Have we done something wrong?" They are both shitting themselves thinking Interpol are on their trail.

"There is no problem; it's just that my father had one just like it; it holds lots of happy memories for me. Where are you going?"

"Oh, we are just touring around; that's the beauty of having a hotel on wheels. We love the freedom of it. We will probably head down towards Spain, but there are no set plans."

"Yes, the freedom of the road. Well, I will let you go. It has been nice meeting you both, and good luck. I hope you have a great trip. I am envious; it's a lovely old camper. When I retire, I am going to get one and just tour all over. Well, that's my plan anyway."

"Well, let's hope you enjoy your retirement touring like us, eh, Jack?"

"Yes, you can't beat it. I am sure you will love it. Well, nice talking to you. Cheers, oh, and by the way, your English is excellent."

"Thanks."

They drive off, getting a wave from the copper.

"Good God, Jack, I don't think my heart will stand much more of this. I thought Interpol was after us. I keep seeing handcuffs flashing before my eyes."

"I know what you mean, mate. The trick is not to panic under pressure. I thought we handled that well. It's just like acting in a film if we can think of it like that. We will keep calm under pressure. Let's get out of here; we have got to be in Spain by tomorrow afternoon. So, we can't fuck about, or we will miss your appointment with the lawyer, and we can't afford to let that happen, or that will have a knock-on effect with all our other business."

Frank and Jack take turns at driving through France at a max speed of 60 mph, constantly looking in the rear-view mirrors for any sign of police cars. They spend a restless night in a campsite just on the French side of the Spanish border. After an early rise, a shower, and tea and toast, they set off to complete the purchase of Frank's dream villa in the sun. After a few pit stops and lots of swearing, they finally arrive at the Villa-de-Frank. Frank's eyes open wide; he cannot believe how grand it is. He couldn't believe after seeing it on a video on a computer screen, how big and magnificent it was in real life.

"Wow, Jack! What a fucking sight for sore eyes! This is incredible. I can't believe how big it is; it's huge. It's like a small castle. What is Mary going to make of this? She won't believe it. I can hardly believe it myself."

They park the camper, walk towards the gates, and press the entrance pad. After a few seconds, the automatic gates start to open, and they are greeted by an immaculately dressed and very distinguished-looking man of about sixty years old wearing a white suit and a Panama hat, and with a perfectly groomed beard. He walks forward towards them, holding out his hand.

"Allow me to introduce myself. I am Don Carlos, the solicitor for the conveyance of this property. Welcome to the Costa del Sol."

They shake hands and introduce themselves.

"Please, gentlemen, bring your vehicle inside, and we will close the gates; we don't want any unexpected guests while we are dealing with this slightly unusual transaction, shall we say? Please come in and meet my distinguished client, Mr

Alfredo Valdez the third. He is one of the bravest and most distinguished bull fighters in the whole of Spain."

The three of them walk into the grand entrance hall to be introduced to Alfredo.

"Alfredo, this is Mr Frank Harrison, the gentleman who is buying your villa."

Alfredo steps forward, clicks his heels together military style and shakes Frank's hand, saying in broken English, "I am pleased for you. I am Alfredo Valdez the third of Spain."

Frank shakes his hand and smiles and says, "I am pleased to meet you, Alf. We have come a long way to meet you. I hope you are well."

Alfredo looks confused at Frank and says, "No, I am Alfredo."

"Sorry, Alfredo, it was my mistake. Let's get on. I am sure you want to get on with it as much as I do. We have got your money, so if all the paperwork is in order, we can complete our transaction quickly. How does that sound?"

The solicitor steps forward at this slightly embarrassing moment and says, "Well, gentlemen, I have the paperwork, which is all in order. If you have the money, we will proceed with the exchange of contracts, and we can all have our celebratory toast to seal the deal, as is our way in Spain. I don't know how you do things in England, but that is our tradition over here in Spain."

Frank lifts the heavy bag onto the huge dining table, opens the bag and pours the money onto the table. Alfredo's eyes light up.

"Yes, it's all here as agreed. Is that okay?" Frank says, looking nervous at this stage.

The solicitor says, "Yes, that's exactly as we agreed on. I am afraid the way the economy in Spain is, we are having to do more and more of these, shall we say, unorthodox types of transactions. Cash is much preferred in a growing number of cases. I am seeing it more and more nowadays. I will count the money while you read the contract. And then I will answer any questions you might have before we finalise things."

"Okay, Don, that makes sense. You will find it easy to count; it's all in thousand-pound bundles straight from the bank."

Don says, "Don't talk to me about banks; they have ruined Spain."

"It's the same in the UK; it's bloody criminal what they have done and got away with. There's a lot of it going on, Don."

Forty-five minutes later, the solicitor says, "Well, everything seems to be in order here. Have you got any questions before we complete the transaction?"

"No, I think everything is fine; you have done a good job from what I can see, very thorough, indeed. This does include 24-hour security for the next six weeks, as I requested?"

"Yes, of course, it's all arranged. Here is a copy of the security's documents for you to keep. They are a first-class, long-established company with a good reputation, and of course, the villa is fully alarmed. The safe has been installed from a company they have recommended. The locksmith, he will be here at nine o'clock in the morning to show you how to set the combination, and he will reset the alarm system with your personal code. Well, Mr Harrison, if you would sign here, and here. and once again over the stamp, please. My client has already signed the document. Thank you, Mr

Harrison, you are now the new owner of this magnificent villa. Now we must finish the deal in the traditional Spanish way with a large glass of sherry to toast the new owner, and then we will leave you in peace. Alfredo has told his housekeeper to make up two en-suite bedrooms before she left, so you can stay as long as you like. Also, there is plenty to eat and drink in the fridges, and you have my card if you need anything when you have moved over here. Please don't hesitate to call me. You can rest assured I will provide you with excellent service. I have lots of UK clients."

Jack says, "Well, Frank Harrison, here's to a happy future in your new home. Cheers." They raise their glasses and drink the sherry down in one.

Alfredo says, "Yes, I hope you enjoy the villa as much as my wife and I enjoyed living here, if it wasn't (shouts) for that bastard, I would kill her…Sorry, sorry. Well, she won't see a euro from me, the bitch! Goodnight, gentlemen. I am off to buy a gun, just joking." He throws his cape over his shoulder and leaves.

Jack looks disturbed and says, "Bloody hell, do you think he really will buy a gun to kill his ex-wife and her lover?"

The solicitor cuts in, "Of course not; he is one of the finest bull fighters in all of Spain. It would be shameful for him to shoot his ex-wife; he would use his sword. Anyway, he only kills bulls, not cows. Just my little joke. Goodbye, gentlemen."

As soon as the door closes, Frank grabs Jack and dances around the room. "Fuck me, Jack, we have done it. That's a million sorted, and what a pad! Mary will wet herself when she finds out this is her home after that poxy flat we have been living in back home, correction, old home. Jack, it's a new start. That woman deserves this after what I have put her through; it takes a special sort of woman to stick with her man through thick and thin. Good job her name isn't Valdez, eh, Jack?"

"Yes, Frank, they have both been amazingly strong; they don't make them like that anymore. If we manage to pull this off, they will have nothing but the best in the future. Let's have a bloody drink, or I will never sleep tonight."

"Bloody good idea, Jack. Where's the kitchen, do you think?"

They find the kitchen, and true to form, Mr Valdez the third has left the fridge full of fine food and a rack of vintage wine. What a great guy he turned out to be!

Both eat and drink the night away. The next morning, Frank walks out onto one of the balconies overlooking the sea, with a glass of water in one hand and two paracetamol in the other. Jack is already there, sitting down, drinking a cup of coffee and reading the paper.

"Morning, Jack. I feel terrible. What time did you get up?"

"About two hours ago. I had bacon and eggs, and then I walked down to the beach to get a paper. Do you want me to get you some breakfast, a nice plate of bacon and eggs?"

"I don't think I could face it; I would be sick. I will have a cup of coffee and a slice of toast; that will do me. I don't know how you manage it. I really don't. You must have the constitution of an elephant; that's all I can say."

"Willpower, Frank, will power and plenty of practice. The locksmith is waiting for you downstairs. I have given him a pot of coffee and some biscuits, but that was half an hour ago. You had better go and sort him out; we don't want him pissing off; we have got to be on our way soon to do the Italian job."

"I don't know about sorting him out. I could do with someone sorting me out first. All right, I am going. I know we have got to get going. I suppose you can't wait to see your new place now you have seen this one."

The locksmith has briefed Frank on all his security matters and left. Jack and Frank empty a mattress of a million and pack it neatly in the safe and close the door. Frank spins the combination wheel.

"Well, that's a good job done, Frank; that's your petty cash tucked away safely. You set the alarm, and we will be on our way. Have you put the deeds in the safe?"

"Yes, they're in there with the readies. I just hope we can get to yours and do your deal without any upsets."

Frank and Jack walk out, locking doors behind them, and walk to the campervan, Frank moaning about his headache. Frank asks Jack, "Are you sure you checked all the windows and doors?"

"Yes, yes, I went around twice; the place is watertight. Don't worry, everything will be okay. They climb aboard and head for the gates that majestically open automatically. They drive out. Frank looks back at his magnificent villa.

"I still can't believe what we are doing," he says as he looks back at his villa. "Come on, Jack, let's go and buy you one. You drive; I will take over later when my head sorts itself out. How far is it to Toby's place, do you think?"

"Well, as near as I can say, about 1,500 miles; it is a bloody good drive, but it will be worth it. We have just got to get stuck in and do it. After driving for 10 hours, they pull into the French town of Montpellier and stop the night in a roadside café car park. They wake up, freshen up and go into the café for breakfast. No sign of a full English, all bloody croissants, pastries, and strong coffee. They can't help overhearing two Italian lorry drivers talking, and they catch the word 'border'.

Frank walks over and enquires.

"Do you speak English?"

"Little, little. How can I help?"

"You were talking about the border. Was it 'the Border' you were talking about?"

"Si, we were saying how. How you say? Strict it has got since they found drug mules. We're crossing from France into Italy. "If you are going into Italy expect a delay at the border."

"Did you hear that, Jack? The Italian border cops are on high alert due to drug trafficking. What a bastard; that's just our luck. That could be curtains for us. What shall we do, Jack?"

"Well, what can we do? We can't turn back now; everything is arranged with Toby and the other lawyer. We will just have to chance it; we have got no choice."

"I suppose you're right; we can't stop now. How far is it to Toby's place from here, do you know?"

Jack looks at his phone.

"Christ, Frank, we have still got over 500 miles to go. Do you think we will get there today?"

"Well, let's think. If we can average 45 miles an hour, that is 12 hours more or less. And we will have to stop from time to time for fuel and have a break; it will be nearer 15 hours. No, it's too much. If we spend 9 hours on the road, that should get us to Nice in the south of France; that's only 30 kilometres, about 25 miles from the French/Italian border. We can stop there for the night and then drive the last leg to

Toby's place the next day, which will only be about 5 or 6 hours. That would make more sense, don't you think?"

"Yes, you're right, Jack; we would be silly to push it. We have got to be sensible. It's imperative that this mission goes smoothly. We can't fuck this up. If all this goes to plan, the job is complete, and we can go home happy. Besides, I have always wanted to go to Nice; we might see some film stars with a bit of luck."

"Yes, Frank, with our sort of luck, it will probably be Mickey Mouse and Donald Duck." They both laugh.

Our knights of the road made it to Nice and spent an uneventful night in Nice. They didn't see any film stars, not even Mickey Mouse or Donald Duck. After having a hearty breakfast, they set off for the next leg of their journey to buy Jack his retirement home on the Italian Riviera. They arrived at the Italian border about 50 minutes later to find a queue; the border guards were spot-checking vehicles.

"Fucking hell, Frank, this could be the end. If they check us, we are finished. I have got an idea: let's put on our fishing hats and lean the rods and nets by the windscreen where they can see them. It might work; it's worth a try."

"Well, anything is worth a try. We can't turn around; there's a fucking massive queue behind us. Hurry up then, jump in the back and sort it; we are moving quite quickly. Faster than I thought we would."

Jack jumps in the back and gets the hats and the fishing gear. A few minutes later, they are driving towards the guard; they both force a smile. The guard smiles back and waves them through.

Jack slumps down in the seat and sighs.

"Fuck me, that was close, Frank. Who's a clever boy, then? I need a drink."

"Jack, I will give you credit; that was a bloody brainwave just when we needed it. Well done. And I will stop at the next bar and buy us both a drink. I am fucking shaking. That guard must be a fisherman; you found his soft spot just when we needed it, thank God. The luck has found us again; all this stress is putting years on me."

After a couple of fuel and drink stops, they drive into Lucca, which is about seven miles from Carrara. They drive into Toby's front yard and toot the horn. Toby and his wife Barbara come out to greet them.

Toby says, "Bonjourno, Jack. Bonjourno, Frank, welcome to Italy. Come in, my friends, come in. You must be tired with all the driving you two have done over the last few days. Especially in that old crate. Park the old bus in the garage and we will lock her up; we wouldn't want to lose the cargo, eh, what? You got through the border without any trouble, then? I was a bit worried. I heard there was a security clampdown, something to do with drugs. Bloody drug dealers, they should lock them up and throw away the bloody key. The world has gone soft, that's the problem; nobody in government has got any balls. Sorry, chaps, but I can't help getting angry about this particular subject; it's because one of my close friend's daughters died from a heroin overdose."

Frank says, "No, Toby, don't apologise. Me and Jack feel the same way. They're evil bastards that sell nothing but misery. I would hang the bastards if I had my way."

They park the old bus, as Toby mockingly referred to it, the cheeky bugger, and walk into the house to be greeted by Toby.

"Well, chaps, sit yourselves down. I will get you a nice, cold gin and tonic, or would you prefer tea? Only joking; I just wanted to see Jack's face drop."

Barbara walks in.

"Is Toby looking after you? You must be exhausted. At least you can have a good night's sleep in a proper bed. I have made up two of the guest rooms for you. Dinner will be ready in about 30 minutes. I will leave you boys to have a good old chat. I suppose you have got a lot to talk about. It's been a long time since you have had a chance to talk face to face. I am sure there is lots to talk about. I keep forgetting how long ago it was when we moved over here; it will be five years next month! I will give you a shout when the dinner is ready." Barbara leaves the room.

"Well, Toby, it's great to see you again. Barbara is right; how the time flies. I don't know about you, but it seems to me the older you get, the faster it bloody well goes."

"I know what you mean, and the constant good weather here doesn't help because every day is the same. Not like dreary old England, where the weather changes every ten minutes."

"You're right there, Toby; England is very dreary at the moment, what with this bloody credit crunch an' all, but don't let's dwell on dreary things. On a light-hearted note, is everything all set for the big buy tomorrow? I can't wait to see my new villa. Pictures on a computer screen are better than nothing, but to see it in the flesh is a completely different ball game."

"Well, Jack, as Barbara said, it will be five years next month since we moved over here; it's the best thing we've ever done. Yes, everything is set for a meeting at the villa at ten o'clock in the morning; it should only take an hour to do the conveyancing. I have got everything in place. It's a bit like old times, Jack. I haven't lost my touch, although things are much more relaxed over here. So how come you are buying the villa with cash? You haven't robbed a bank, have you, Jack?" Toby laughs.

"No, Toby, nothing that exciting. Me and Frank have tucked away all our cash jobs over the last twenty-five years and sold a couple of bits of land for cash. We didn't want the dirty taxman getting his paws on it. They have had their fair share of us over the years, as you know, so we don't feel guilty about our little sideline, do we, Frank?"

"I'll drink to that. Lovely drop of gin, by the way, Toby."

"I can take a hint. How about you, Jack? Silly question. Give me your glasses, you pair of scoundrels. You don't change, do you? We have had some fun over the years, Jack. I am really looking forward to having you living just down the road from me. I will enjoy showing you around and introducing you to all my friends and, of course, contacts that I have made over the years, some jolly useful ones I can tell you."

Toby serves the drinks on a typically posh silver tray. He sits down and says, "I think you and Wendy will love it out here: lots of fresh air, excellent locally produced food and wine and plenty of sunshine, and your villa looks magnificent. It puts this place to shame. Mind you, once you have settled in over here, you can remodel this place for me. You have got a real talent for design, Jack. I remember looking at some of your houses over the years; they were stunning. No wonder you scooped all those builder of the year awards. I think you must have won more awards than any of the big boys. And you got the chance to meet all the celebrities when you went to the Savoy to collect them every year. Do you remember showing me that photograph of you with Barbara Windsor on your lap? You two really knew how to build houses. There was nobody better than P.L.H. when it came to style and innovation."

Frank says, "Well, thanks for that, Toby; it's nice to have a bit of praise for a change. We haven't had much of that lately. Yes, we certainly had our moments, but a lot of water has gone under the bridge since then."

Jack says, "Well, Toby, if everything you say about the area is true, it sounds like we are both going to like living here. You should get a job with the Tourist Board; they could use blokes like you. It will be a pleasure helping you out with this place, but you must keep it to yourself. I am coming out here to retire. I don't want all your mates bothering me to remodel their villas."

"Okay, you have got a deal, Jack; mum's the word. I think you and Wendy will settle in here very quickly. There are lots of retired Brits living locally from all walks of life, mainly ex-businessmen and women. There's a fair amount of retired military folk as well, generals, admirals. There's even a wing commander. I have the odd round of golf with Sandy; that's his nickname. Apparently he crash-landed on a beach somewhere in France, hence the name. They are all proper old-school types, and of course Barbara will introduce Wendy to all her friends. There is always something going on; we have lots of gatherings, parties, that sort of thing. I think once you settle in, you will wish you had come out here years ago."

Barbara calls, "Dinner is served. Would you like to come through and bring your drinks with you?"

There is lots of small talk over dinner. They enjoyed a wonderful offering of lamb with all the trimmings, complemented by some excellent local wines. All slept well. The next morning after a light breakfast, Toby, Frank, and Jack set off to meet the vendor and his solicitor at his office with a suitcase fully loaded with one million smackers, the agreed amount for the purchase of the villa in Carrara. On arrival, they were introduced to Giovanni, the solicitor, and Roberto, the vendor, who unfortunately spoke very little English. In just over an hour, the deal was completed, contracts were exchanged, and Jack was the new owner of a brand-new villa overlooking the sea. They all went into the property for the official handover and gave Jack the keys and combinations to the safe and security system. When they have finished the grand tour, Roberto shakes hands with Jack, and looking like a cat that had got the double cream, he rabbits on in fluent Italian, and the only word that kept coming up that they could understand was *Grazie*. And at that, he left whistling as he went. Jack asked Giovanni what was that all about.

Giovanni said, "He was trying to say how grateful he was that you had bought the villa. He has been trying to sell it for a long time, and I happen to know the bank was going to, how you say, make him bankrupt. The house builders around here are going through hard times now; that's why he was so happy."

"So let me get this straight. You are saying that my deal saved him from going out of business?"

"Yes, that is correct, Mr Redman; you saved him from bankruptcy."

"Well, I never…God moves in mysterious ways, and that's a fact!"

"Anyway, gentlemen, I must get on. I have got another appointment waiting for me at the office, so I will bid you farewell, and I wish you good luck in your new home."

Jack shakes his hand and thanks him for doing a smooth transaction.

Toby says, "Well, that all went very smoothly, thank God; it does get complicated sometimes with the language problem and all. That was quite a coincidence, Roberto being a builder. You will have to keep in touch with him; good builders are scarce around here. Well, I will have to leave you chaps to it. I have promised to do a bit of shopping for Barbara. I will see you back at my place later. So, lock up and set your alarm, but you needn't worry; there is no crime around here. But I will keep an eye on it until you and Wendy move in."

"Cheers, Toby, you are a good friend. I couldn't have done this without your help. Give me your bill later and I will square you up."

"Don't be silly, old man. I am retired. I didn't do it for money. I just wanted to help a friend. In fact, I rather enjoyed doing it. You can pay me back by remodelling my villa when you get over here. And maybe we can get Roberto to do the work."

"Well, thanks a million, Toby; it will be the best remodelling job I have ever done; I guarantee it. See you later."

Toby leaves and Jack says, "Well, we have done it, Frank; that's another million invested in bricks and mortar. I can't believe that Roberto was about to go under. How ironic is that? We rob a bank in England and save a builder we have never met before with the cash. I am not a great believer in fate, but what were the chances? Anyway, let's stash the cash in the safe and get locked up and get away. Just one more link in the chain now, Frank. Please, Lord, let's get it done without any problems. How much are you taking home with you?"

"Six grand. That should be plenty. If the Swiss connection works out, we should have access to legitimate money. How about you, Jack?"

"That sounds about right. I will do the same. We will spend the night at Toby's place and leave fresh first thing in the morning. Not too much wine tonight, eh, Frank?"

They get back to Toby's at about four o'clock to kill a bit of time before dinner. Jack and Frank measure the house so that Jack can draw up the remodelling plans when they are back in England.

The next morning after a good night's sleep and a full English breakfast, they prepare to drive out of the yard. Jack winds down the window and says, "Thanks again, Toby, and you, Barbara, you have been great."

"Bye, you two. I have packed you some lunch and some drinks; it's in the fridge. I hope you enjoy it. And have a safe journey home."

"Thanks, Barbara. I hope so, and thanks for doing our packed lunch; we do appreciate it. We are a bit lost without our wives; it's nice to be looked after."

Toby turns to Jack and says, "Yes, have a safe journey, and don't worry about the villa. I have asked my friend, the chief of police, to ask the night shift to keep a close eye on it. He is looking forward to meeting you, Jack."

"Cheers! That will be nice." They drive off.

Jack says, "The chief of fucking police! That's all I fucking need. Although thinking about it, if he is a friend of Toby's, he must be bent, or Toby wouldn't have become a friend of his."

"Yeh, I'm sure you're right, Jack. Toby would stay well clear of him if he wasn't, and he might be a good contact to have. Like Toby said, things are a lot more relaxed over here anyway. He wouldn't introduce you to anyone that could cause you any grief. Toby's no fool; he is a shrewd old feller; he definitely wouldn't put you in the firing line with anybody."

"Yeh, well, time will tell. Right, let's get to Switzerland and see this dodgy banker our Jay has sorted out for us. I hope he turns out to be a winner. This is going to be fucking risky. I just hope Jay has found us a good banker, not a bent wanker."

After a long day's drive passing through the Mont Blanc Tunnel from Italy into France, they arrive and book in at a campsite, which is about five miles from the Swiss border near Geneva. After finishing the food that Barbara prepared for them, washed down with some fine Italian wine, Jack phones his son Jay.

"Hi, Jay, me and your Uncle Frank have arrived in France. We are at a campsite called Bord-De-Rivière; it's just outside Ferney-Voltaire, where you used to live. Can you come over? It's important that we get on with it; time is getting tight for us getting back to England."

"Yes, I will leave now. I will see you in about an hour. I am looking forward to seeing you and Uncle Frank. This all seems a bit strange. Anyway, I can't wait to see you both. It's been a long time since I have seen you both together. You have always had holidays at separate times so that one of you can run the firm while the other one is away."

Just over an hour later, Jay arrives at the campervan; he parks his car and gets out. Jack and Frank walk out to meet him. After a few hugs, they go into the camper for a chat. They sit down, and Frank pours three glasses of wine.

Jay says, "Well, are you going to tell me how you came by this fortune in cash now that we are face to face? Come on, Dad, spill the beans."

"Well, it is quite simple, son. We robbed a bank in London, and that is the truth. Now I have told you, you must never tell a soul, or your Uncle Frank and me could end up doing a long prison sentence. And I am sure you wouldn't want that on your conscience for the rest of your life."

"I can't believe you two old buggers. How did you manage to pull off a bank job? You have got bloody nerve; I will give you that! I just can't imagine you two as villains that rob banks. How did you get away with something you don't know anything about?"

Frank cuts in, "Planning, Jay; we planned every step meticulously. We developed a no clues, no convictions policy. It took us months; it started off with your dad telling me about a bloke he met in a pub who was in the flying squad in London. He told him it could be done if it was planned right. But at first, I was dead against it. I thought your dad was having some sort of breakdown due to the pressure we were under with the business being in the shit. We had everybody and his dog chasing us for money. So I went along with it just as a plan to help your dad get through the trauma of the business going down the pan. I never dreamt we would actually do it, but you know how persuasive your dad can be; he has got a master's degree in bullshit. So, what started off as a distracting pastime grew into reality; we both have a job believing it. It just seems like a vague memory because it was six months ago when we did it."

"Yes, son, that's about how it happened. It just grew on us; it seemed like it wasn't real, and then one day, it was. We just did it like a couple of robots; we have often said we can't believe we did it. We waited for things to settle down for six months. We had the money in an old water tank under Frank's shed down at his allotment; how daft is that! Anyway, here we are. Can you help us, son? We are desperate to get this money into a Swiss bank so that we can finally relax and get back home."

"I can help, but I don't want to get involved in any way; I told you that when you phoned me. I will give you the number of a senior bank manager in the business sector. You will contact him directly, and he will do the job for you. He will want between 3 and 5% of whatever you bank with him. But at least the money will be legit and making you interest.

Here's his business card. His name is Edward Knight; it's on the card with his private mobile phone number."

"Thanks, son. I hope he is all right, this wanker of a banker of yours. You won't regret this, son. I will make it worth your while, and you and your missus and the kids can spend your holidays with me and your mum at the villa."

"Villa? What fucking villa? You didn't say anything about a villa?"

"Oh, sorry, son, forgot to mention it. I have bought a six-bedroom villa with a swimming pool on the Italian Riviera. Frank's done the same in Spain."

"You pair of old villains amaze me! I can't believe what I am hearing. Does Mum know what you two have been up to?"

"No, of course she doesn't. She thinks me and your Uncle Frank are on a fishing trip in France. So, keep your mouth shut. It's very important that she doesn't know anything about any of this at this stage. I don't want her worrying until I know everything is safely tied up. So, you must promise me that you won't breathe a word, okay?"

"Yes, of course, I promise. You can trust me, you know that."

"Yes, I know that. I just hope we can trust your banker. We keep getting strange things happening, and now this. We do daylight robbery, and now there's a man called Knight rinsing our dodgy dosh. Well, it's a strange world, all right and no mistake. Look at you, being in the right place at the right time; it's all so bloody strange."

"Don't worry, you can trust Edward. What is it they say, honour among thieves? And he is a Freemason in my lodge. I still can't believe you two buggers have robbed a bank. Come on, I will take you out for a drink in the camp bar. I have been here before when I lived in Ferney-Voltaire. It is a really well-run site, and the bar serves good food, and you can get your breakfast there in the morning."

Frank pours another three glasses of wine and proposes a toast.

"Here's to all of us; may we live as long as we can and die when we can't help it. Cheers." They all laugh and take a drink.

The next morning in the campervan, Jack picks up his phone, a bit shaky with nerves and the drink from the night before.

"What do you think, Frank? Do you think we can trust this banker bloke? After what we have been through, it's bloody hard to trust anybody in the banking world. Come on, Frank, what do you think?"

"Well, as I see it, we haven't got an alternative, so make the call."

"Now be serious, Frank. Are you sure? This is the most important part of the job getting the money laundered, so we don't have to duck and dive for the rest of our bloody lives. If this bit goes wrong, we have done all this for half the original haul."

"Well, I am sure your Jay wouldn't hook us up with this guy if he wasn't a hundred percent sure it would be okay. Jay has worked in finance over here for eight years; he must know this bloke well enough to trust him to handle our delicate financial situation. And don't forget Edward is going to get a bloody good pay day out of the deal."

"Yes, you're right, Frank. Jay wouldn't have set it up with this Edward character if he wasn't confident he could do the business for us."

Jack looks at Edward's business card and rings the main bank number, to make sure that he really is a senior bank manager.

A lady answers with a posh English accent.

"Good morning, LNDS Banking Services. How may I help?"

"I would like to speak to Edward Knight; he is the senior bank manager at your branch, I believe."

"Yes, that is correct. Is he expecting your call? He is a very busy man."

"Yes, he is. Tell him it's Mr Redman. I am sure he will squeeze me into his busy schedule."

"I will see if he is available to take your call; please hold the line."

Jack listens to some shitty music for a few nervous minutes, then the posh voice returns.

"I am putting you through, Mr Redman."

"Good morning, Mr Redman. I have been expecting your call. I suggest we meet at the Metropolitan Hotel at the rooftop bar at lunchtime at, shall we say, one o'clock. I will be wearing a grey suit with a red tie. Would that be all right with you and Mr Harrison?"

"That will be fine with us; we look forward to meeting you there. Cheers, Mr Knight."

"Yes, and I will look forward to meeting you two fellows; your son has told me a lot about you both. All good, might I add. See you at one then. Goodbye."

Jack turns to Frank. "That seemed to go well; so far so good, eh? I suppose time will tell, but I think Jay has got us a good contact. We had better get dressed up; this rooftop bar sounds posh to me."

"I am sure it will be, Jack. He doesn't sound like the sort of bloke that would arrange a business meeting in Wetherspoons, do you?" They both laugh.

Later that morning, they are driving towards the Swiss border with the money packed in suitcases, very nervous as they approach the guardhouse. The guard steps out when he sees the UK number plates. Jack winds the window down, shitting himself but doing a good impersonation of a swan.

The guard says, "Please state where you are going and what the reason for your visit to Switzerland is, and can I see your passports, please?"

"Oh, we are visiting my son and his family, and we are hoping to do a bit of fishing if that's possible."

The guard walks around and slides open the door and looks in; he sees the fishing gear and slides the door closed.

"Okay, have a nice visit. I am a fisherman. I fish the lake when I can. You will enjoy fishing here. Drive on and have a good vacation, and don't do anything I wouldn't do."

Jack drives on and sighs loudly. "Let's just hope this Edward guy gets our money into his bank. I don't fancy going through any more borders with it; our luck is bound to run out one day. My nerves are about shattered."

"Fucking hell, that could have gone wrong. It's a good job he is a fisherman. Well, you could say he took the bait, eh, Jack? Don't do anything he wouldn't do, if only he knew he had just let two bank robbers into the country with 4.5 million quid in stolen notes."

"Well, he didn't, Frank, and let's thank God he didn't."

It is 12:50 pm. Jack and Frank have arrived at the Metropolitan Hotel. They grab the lift and go to the rooftop bar; it is very posh as they suspected, and bustling with business types. It's now one o'clock, and they are both looking around for the man in the grey suit with a red tie.

Frank says, "That's him at the bar, I think."

Jack says, "Hang on, Frank, that guy sitting over there is dressed the same. Bollocks, what do we do now?"

"I have got an idea, Jack. Go over near the one at the bar and discreetly drop the business card that Jay gave you then pick it up and ask him if he dropped it, and if he says it isn't his, we know it's the other guy."

"A cunning plan, you crafty old bugger. Go on then, off you go."

"No, Jack, you are better at things like that than me; you have got the cheek of old Nick. Anyway, you have got the card, go on, hurry up."

"All brains and no fucking bottle, that's you all over, Frank. Right, I will do it. Here goes."

Jack walks over and carefully drops the card and picks it up.

"Is this your card? I think you dropped it when you took your wallet out."

"Yes, as a matter of fact, it is, and you must be Mr Redman if I am not mistaken."

"Yes, but please call me Jack."

"Likewise, call me Edward. Now what can I get you and your colleague to drink?"

"Two pints of lager would be nice, Edward, if that's okay."

They get their drinks and walk out onto the roof terrace overlooking Lake Geneva; they sit down at a quiet table well out of earshot of anybody.

"Well, it's nice to meet you both. Jack, you are Jay's father aren't you, you should be very proud of him he is a lovely guy. We have done quite a few deals together over the years. He has become a personal friend as well as a business associate. I don't know if he has mentioned it, but we are both in the same Masonic Lodge here in Geneva. That's why when he asked me to help you, I said I would. Well, first, may I say what you are asking me to do is very risky indeed. I will have to create a dummy company in China that I will put all the money into and immediately transfer it into our bank, and that way it will look like a legitimate Chinese company has decided to use our bank. You two will be the only two directors, then I will open two accounts one each, then I will immediately close the company down and transfer the money equally into your two accounts. This can all be done in two trading days. So how much are we intending to bank?"

Frank says, "Four million pounds, two million each. And your commission, of course, which you can have in cash if that suits you?"

"That's quite a lot to get through unnoticed. But I can do it; it will cost you five percent of the 4 million, which means my commission will be 200 thousand pounds, and yes, cash will be fine. Is that okay with you guys?"

Jack bursts out, "That sounds a bit fucking strong if you don't mind me saying so, Edward."

"Well, you can take it or leave it. I will be taking a great risk by helping you guys."

Jack retorts, "Not as big a risk as we took getting it in the first place."

"I take your point, Jack; it does sound a lot, I agree, but I can assure you, I will earn every franc of my commission.

And I will personally manage your accounts, making sure they earn high interest, around 5% on average, from day one. So, do we have a deal or not?"

Jack says, "Can we have a moment, Edward?"

"Of course you can; it's a big decision, but don't take too long. I must get back to the bank in twenty minutes or so."

Jack turns to Frank and walks him away to talk.

"What do you think, Frank? I think we can trust him. What do you think?"

"Well, if Jay said he was trustworthy. Fuck it, let's do it."

Both go back and shake hands with Edward.

Jack says, "Okay, Eddie boy, we are in. So how do you propose we complete this clandestine operation?"

"When I go back to my office, I will make an appointment for you at 4:30 this afternoon; that is my last appointment of the day. You bring the consignment, including my commission, and we will count the money together. I will work late tonight. I will put the money on and off the market electronically. I will make a second appointment for you both at 4:30 tomorrow afternoon, whereupon I will present you with the necessary paperwork, debit cards, credit cards, etc. I will need both your addresses and some kind of ID."

Jack grabs Edward's lapel and pulls him over the table.

"It all sounds great. But get this quite clear: for around twenty hours, we have got to trust you with four and a half million pounds. So, let's make it clear that if you try and fuck with us, we will fuck with you. Do you understand, Edward?"

"Now then, Jack, I have been in banking in Geneva most of my adult life. I am respected and revered throughout the Swiss banking world. I can assure you, Jack, that I will not, as you so crudely put it, fuck with you. I will be perfectly happy with the commission that we have agreed upon. Which, might I add, is a fair payment for me risking the reputation I have forged over all my years in banking."

"I am sorry, Edward; it's just the nerves kicking in. You have got to look at it from our point of view. This money represents our security for the rest of our lives; it's just nerves. Once you have legitimised the money, we can relax. Neither of us has had much sleep since we left England."

"Understood, Jack, but I can assure you that you are in good hands; your son will vouch for that. Well, it was nice, if not a bit scary, meeting you both. I will see you both at the bank later this afternoon at 4:30. Oh, and don't come in the main entrance; there is a side door to the left of the main entrance. It wouldn't look good, you two walking in with suitcases."

Jack says, "Good thinking, Edward; we will be there promptly at 4:30."

Edward says his goodbyes and leaves Frank and Jack at the rooftop bar. "Don't forget, 4:30, side door."

Frank grabs Jack's attention.

"Fuck me, Jack, you ripped into him a bit strong. I thought you were going to frighten him off. That could have ruined everything; it was a hell of a risk."

"I was only kidding, but I wanted him to know that we weren't a soft touch. You must bear in mind we are putting a massive amount of trust in somebody we have only known for less than an hour. I didn't want him to think we were a pair of pussies that would roll over if he double-crossed us."

"I suppose you are right, but it was a risky move. It is a hell of a risk, but it's the best option that we have got to clean the money up. Although I can't believe we are trusting our lives with a bank manager after what we have been through with the bastards."

That afternoon at 4:25, they arrive at the side door of the bank and press the intercom button. The lady's posh voice came on.

"Push the door and come in, please." She shows them through to Edward's palatial office. Edward is sitting in a throne-like chair at a huge, carved mahogany desk. He looks most distinguished with his expensive suit, silver hair, and gold-rimmed glasses.

Jack whispers to Frank, "That was easy getting in here; it's a pity we didn't have the guns with us." Frank smiles.

"Hello, gentlemen, or not so gentle in Jack's case! Well, please take a seat. Would you like a coffee or champagne?"

"Coffee would be nice. How about you, Jack?"

"Yes, coffee. Maybe champagne tomorrow, hey, Edward?"

"Yes, that would be more appropriate; we will definitely crack a bottle of bubbly tomorrow."

Edward phones Angela to order the coffee.

"Right, gentlemen, please fill in the forms on the desk, and we will get things moving. Then we will empty the cases and count the money."

Angela comes in with a silver tray with the coffee and a fine assortment of biscuits, then leaves. After some small talk about the weather and exchanging pleasantries about their families over coffee and biscuits, they empty the cases. While Frank and Jack fill in the forms. Edward starts to weigh the notes. After 20 minutes, Edward says, "Well, it is exactly as you said: 4.3 million pounds, and my 200 thousand pounds commission for me. You will both have £2,150,000 each in your new accounts by tomorrow. So, everything is in order; don't worry, you have my word on it."

Edward checks their forms and examines their passports for ID.

"Well, that all looks in order, gentlemen. When you come in tomorrow at 4:30, you will be legitimate millionaires. How will that feel, do you think?"

Frank replies, "That will feel great. Me and Jack haven't slept very well since we acquired the bloody money; it will be a great relief to know it's safe in a Swiss bank."

"Yes, as Frank said, it will be great to know the money is safe. It has been nerve-racking having it with us, especially going through so many bloody borders. It's been a hell of a journey, but hopefully, we can relax a bit more now. Although no disrespect to you, Edward, I will feel better when our business is concluded tomorrow, then we can really relax and enjoy that glass of champagne you offered earlier."

"I am sure you will; you are bound to be worried as this is a most unorthodox negotiation we are having, but I can assure you everything will be fine; you're not the first to come to Switzerland with a lot of money to, what shall we say, tidy up. Although that is an awful lot of money to be carrying around. I am amazed it wasn't seized at one of the borders. You were very lucky to get through all those borders without getting caught; the odds of you getting away with that would be remarkably low. Over the years, I have heard of many cases that have had money confiscated crossing one border, and you guys crossed five; that must be a record! Lady Luck must have been your passenger. Well, I look forward to seeing you tomorrow afternoon. Angela will show you out."

Frank and Jack leave the bank and go back to the campervan, feeling relieved but anxious. Jack says, "I still don't know if we can trust that bastard; it seems crazy leaving him with all that money without so much as a receipt. If he denied all knowledge of us ever giving it to him, what the fuck could we do?"

"What else can we do, Jack? It couldn't stay under my shed forever, and if Edward does the business for us, we will be safe; it's the grand finish to the perfect job. I still can't believe we have done it either; it is a hell of a risk. We must rely on Jay's judgement of the man. What else can we do? Well, we aren't going to get much sleep tonight! That's for sure. Let's hope that the Lady Luck that Edward referred to is still riding with us. It's all in God's hands now, Jack."

"Well, Frank, as long as it isn't in our friend Edward's fucking hands, that's all right, but I can't help having my doubts about him; it must be an awful temptation for him to resist."

They drive out of the city to a lakeside picnicking area just outside the pretty little village of Ferney-Voltaire, where they camp for the night. They walk into the village, where they find a good restaurant. After eating a very tasty meal washed down with some strong German beer, they return to the camper for a very restless night. The next morning, they awake with the sun streaming through the window. They go to the toilet block for a shit, shower, shave, and shampoo. Then they head into the Village Café for breakfast. To kill time, they decide to break out the fishing tackle and try their luck in the lake. They catch a steady stream of fish, mostly small ones, but it still distracts them from the main feature of the day: Edward

Knight and Co. A couple of hours later, it is time for them to go and face their fears.

They arrive at the bank just before 4:30.

They are shown into Edward's office by the posh voice lady Angela to be greeted by Edward with the traditional handshake.

"Good afternoon, gentlemen, please take a seat. I trust you slept well with our wonderful Swiss mountain air to breathe."

"Not really, did we, Jack? We were worried about our money, to be honest. It felt very odd giving it to you without any paperwork to prove we had. It's not the sort of thing you do these days, what with all the scams that go on. Trust is a thing of the past, I am afraid; well, it is in England anyway. I don't know about over here."

"No need to have worried. You are now, as I promised, legitimate millionaires. Jack, here are your debit and credit cards, gold, of course, and here are yours, Frank. Both of your accounts are up and running and making interest as of today. You can breathe easy now. How does that feel?"

Jack says loudly, "Great, fucking great! What relief! We were thinking all sorts could go wrong. Edward, I misjudged you, and I apologise for that, but you have got to bear in mind the way the banks have treated us in England; the word bank manager immediately sends us into suspicion mode. By the way, Edward, what is the limit on our credit cards, do you know?"

"There is no real limit, Jack; you have £2,150,000 in each of your accounts, which is accruing interest at 5%. Do you realise how much that is? Surely you have worked it out by now?"

"No, I didn't like to tempt fate by assuming everything would go to plan with the bulk of our money. So how much is it, Edward?"

Edward picks up a calculator and hits the buttons at high speed and says, "Well, Jack, that works out in round figures if you add compound interest at around two thousand eight hundred to three thousand of your GBP pounds a week. If you put the bank app on your phone, you can see your balance at the touch of a button. Your money will make approximately four hundred pounds a day, and there will be interest on interest, which is why I can't give you a more precise figure. How does that sound, gentlemen?"

Jack says, "Edward, I would like to shake your hand and reiterate my apology to you. I must confess I was very wary of trusting you. But you have certainly turned out to be a man of your word. You have my greatest admiration; you really do. We will never be able to thank you enough."

Frank says, "I second that, Edward. I can't wait to try out the cards. Well done, Edward, you have done us a great service. It's a big thank you from both me and Jack. So, let's have that glass of champagne you promised us. I think we all deserve a celebratory drink, don't you?"

"Of course, of course we do." Edward presses the intercom and askes Angela to bring in a bottle of the best bubbly. Edward pops the cork, and they all drink a toast to success and happiness. A few minutes later, all three walk to the door.

Edward smiles and remarks, "Although I have never met you, it has been a pleasure not knowing you, and it will be a pleasure to continue not knowing you." They all laugh.

"Well, Edward, me and Jack will wholeheartedly agree with that, and it will be nice not knowing you for years to come. Only kidding! It's been a privilege dealing with you; it's refreshing to deal with an honest banker for a change."

On their way out, they ask posh Angela to put the bank app on their phones. While she is doing that, they have a brief chat in the corridor.

Jack says, "What was all that bullshit you was giving Edward about being an honest banker? He is about as honest as the great train robbers. Anyway, Franky boy, may I buy you a drink? I think I can afford it, don't you?"

"Why not? I think another celebratory drink would be well in order."

Jack and Frank thank Angela for putting the app on their phones and leave the bank. They make their way back to where they have parked the campervan. They go into a five-star hotel bar. Frank orders two large brandies and flashes the gold card. They sit on the bar stools and have a chat.

Frank says, "We have done it; we have bloody done it. I can't believe it; we are bloody legal millionaires. We have completed the perfect bank robbery. Two builders who were bankrupt six months ago and now we are legally rich. And we saved another builder in another country from going bust as well. What a shame we can't brag about it. If they gave awards for bank robbers, we would take first prize. Jack, I thought you were mad when you started going on about it, but I'm bloody glad I let you talk me into it."

"I can't believe it either, Frank. I have got you to thank for this. You trusted me, and you never let me down. I would never have done it if it wasn't for you, mate. And you were right; we were bloody good bank robbers. I am going to miss you, Frank."

"Same here, Jack. It's been a long road we have travelled together, and we have been mates for thirty years. It will seem very strange not having you around. It's something we never considered until now. I am sure we will stay in touch somehow."

"Yeh, I am sure we will. Well, now we have done what we came here to do; we had better think of heading home. We will spend tonight here and set off early tomorrow; we can do it in a day if we take it in turns driving and keep going."

"Phone your Jay and invite him and his missus out to dinner on me. That's the least we can do. Jay played a blinder finding Edward for us; we couldn't have done it without his help."

"That's nice of you, Frank. Are you sure you can afford it?" They both laugh.

That evening, they all went to a posh restaurant on Jay's recommendation and enjoyed an expensive meal on Frank.

The next morning after the first good night's sleep they have had in a long time, they go to Manor, which is a big department store with a rooftop food hall that serves great self-service breakfasts. After breakfast, they buy a couple of modest presents for their respective wives. A bottle of Chanel No 5 for Wendy, and Frank buys Christian Dior for Mary. They daren't spend too much, or they might wonder where the money came from. No clues, no convictions still applies.

They walk back to the car park, and climb in their faithful old camper, or should it be referred to as their battle wagon? They set off for the long drive home. Thankfully, the journey goes without incident, and they get back exhausted but elated.

They are back in one piece, and the mission was accomplished successfully. The two unsuspecting wives were delighted with their gifts. And both were glad to have their husbands back. The news that they had won ten thousand pounds between them was just as welcome, neither of them knowing that that was just a drop in the ocean compared to what was to come.

Three weeks later, both Jack and Frank have given notice on their rented flats unbeknown to their wives. They have informed social services that they have got jobs in a warehouse.

They have booked flights to Spain and Italy from Heathrow. The flights are on the same morning, thirty minutes apart.

Jack meets Frank in the Bull for a chat.

"Well, Frank, the flights are all set for Saturday the 14th. So how do we tell the girls that we are going away?"

"Let's take them out to dinner and tell them that we have got a surprise for them. We will tell them we have finally got our redundancy cheques, that we have cashed them and that we have booked a surprise holiday for both of us."

"I like it, Frank; it sounds plausible enough to me. They should be well chuffed with the idea. But do you think we should tell them as soon as we get to our villas that we own them, and do we cough about the bank job, or do we tell the tale about fiddling the taxman for twenty-five years like we told Toby? I am not sure they will enjoy their holiday if we confess to the job. What do you think?"

"I see what you mean, Jack. Well, I think let them enjoy the two weeks' holiday and then tell them when they start packing that they needn't bother because they are already home. And then we tell them we have made enough by fiddling the taxman and selling land for cash, we have put by enough into a fund for our retirement plan. What do you think?"

"Well, I think you're right; we won't tell them until the end of the holiday. I think you're right about not telling them about the bank job. I think that would spook them. But will they believe we could have squirreled away enough to live on for the rest of our lives? Especially as we can pretty well spend as much as we like. It's a bit of a dilemma all right; it's something we need to sleep on. I will meet you at ten in the morning at the allotment shed for a final board meeting on the matter."

The next morning in the makeshift boardroom, over a cup of tea, it was decided that they would tell their wives at the end of the two weeks about owning the villas, and not admit to the bank job until it became obvious that they were living above their apparent means. By this time they would be so used to their way of life and feeling quite safe and settled, so they would be more equipped to accept it as it wouldn't come as a complete shock. It would be the slowly, slowly catch the monkey approach to the situation. Decision made, board meeting closed, no minutes taken.

It's now Saturday the 14th; both couples are sitting together at the Costa coffee shop at Heathrow, waiting for their flights.

Wendy says, "I can't believe we are really going on holiday. I didn't think we would ever go on a proper holiday again. You boys do come up with some real surprises. Whatever next?"

Frank says, "Don't be daft; it's the least we could do after what we have put you two through. Life is full of surprises. I am sure we will have lots of holidays in the future. Just wait and see."

Wendy pipes up, "Yes, Jack, and I think I have just seen some pigs landing on runway 2!" They all laugh.

"Yes, I know what you mean, sweetheart, but just let's go and enjoy this one for now; who knows what the future holds? We might win the lottery, who can tell."

Mary says, "I don't think so; we have all been doing it from the start, and we haven't won it yet, so I wouldn't hold your breath on that one if I were you. Anyway, let's start with the next two weeks, and we will take it from there, shall we?"

Last call for Jack and Wendy's flight.

"Come on, Jack, that's the last call. We have got to hurry."

Everyone get up and exchange kisses and hugs.

Mary says, "Have a good time, you two. See you soon."

Wendy says, "Yes, and you. See you in two weeks. Have fun; you deserve it."

Frank looks at Jack.

"Well, this is it, my old mate; you're off."

"Yeh, this is it, Frank, after all these years."

Frank can't help himself. He hugs Jack and whispers, "Look after yourself. I'll miss you, Jack; it's been a great partnership."

Jack whispers back, "And you, Frank; it won't be the same without you, mate."

Wendy interrupts, "Come on, you daft buggers, anybody would think you were never going to see each other again."

Jack and Wendy walk away. Frank stands staring at Jack like a lost child. Jack turns and waves at Frank. Frank struggles to lift his arm and gives a feeble wave back.

Mary sits down with Frank and says, "Now then, Frank, what's the matter?"

"Oh, nothing, Mary, just seeing them two walking away and how close we are, it upset me a bit; that's all it was."

"Well, cheer up, we are going on a long holiday."

Frank thinks, *You don't know how long, Mary. We have gained a lot, but we have lost a lot at the same time.*

Jack and Wendy arrive in Carrara by taxi. They walk towards the gates of the villa. Jack takes the remote out of his pocket and presses the button; the gates open to reveal the magnificent villa. Wendy's jaw drops. Jack grabs Wendy around the waist.

"You know when we were talking at the airport, you told me that you and Frank are always coming up with surprises. Well, this is another surprise."

Meanwhile, Frank and Mary arrive at their Spanish villa. As they walk up the drive, Frank says, "Do you remember what Jack said at Heathrow? He said you never know what's around the corner. Well, this is what's around your corner. We told you that you will enjoy your holiday, so we thought we would push the boat out for you both; you deserve it."

For the next two weeks, Frank and Mary enjoy themselves, wining and dining in the local taverns and restaurants, and swimming in their own pool. It was heaven until the last day. Frank goes in the bedroom to find Mary sitting on the bed with open suitcases at her feet, crying.

Frank kneels and holds her hands and says,

"Mary, my darling, cheer up, Jack and Wendy will be in exactly the same position as us. We are all in this together. Dry your eyes and come downstairs, leave the packing for now."

"I know we are, Frank, but leaving this place to go back to that dreary old flat in England; it just upsets me, that's all it is. I will be all right; don't worry about me. I bet Wendy is feeling just the same; it does break your heart when you think if the firm hadn't gone down, we could have retired to a place like this."

"I know, but try not to upset yourself. I am going to get Jack and Wendy on WhatsApp on my laptop. Dry your eyes and come down when you are ready."

Frank gets Jack on his computer.

"Hi, Jack, is Mary around?"

"No, she is down by the pool, tidying up, ready to leave."

"How is she?"

"Well, she has gone a bit quiet on me. I think she is upset about going back to England. We have had such a good time for the last two weeks that she is struggling just thinking about it. But we know what is going to get their smiles back, don't we, Frank?"

"We certainly do. I don't think they will believe it at first. I will leave it to you; you tell a better story than me."

"Okay, I will call Wendy in, you get Mary sitting with you at the laptop, and I will spring the trap. Ring me back in five minutes."

Five minutes later, they open the laptop and ring in. For the first five minutes, the girls are hogging most of the conversation telling each other about what a great time they have had, how fantastic it has been to have lived in such great surroundings, and what it's like having their own pool to swim in whenever the fancy takes them. Jack is listening carefully, waiting for the right moment to get them screaming. Eventually, Wendy says, "Well, Mary, it's back to reality tomorrow."

Jack intervenes, "Well, ladies, can I get a word in, that is if you don't mind?" They both go quiet. "Thank you. Do you remember when we were at Heathrow and you said we were full of surprises? Well, there is something Frank and I want you to do for us."

Mary says, "And what is that, Jack the Joker? What are you going to pull out of the hat now that will cheer us up!"

"Well, I would like you both to throw away the suitcases."

Wendy says, "And why would we do that silly bloody thing, Jack?"

"Because we ain't going nowhere, and Jack is not joking for once. We own these villas, and that is not a joke." Silence.

THE END